Praise for

At A Loss For Words

"*At A Loss For Words* is another compelling (and hilarious!) expression of Governor General's Award winner Diane Schoemperlen's gift for building the minutiae of everyday life into a profound understanding of women, men, love, and imagination." —*Chatelaine*

"Singularly evocative. . . . A critically praised, consistently fine, lively writer." —*Ottawa Citizen*

"As Schoemperlen holds the mirror up to us, we can't help but see that love is always archetypal and banal at the same time." —*National Post*

"A work of wry twists and subtle surprises. . . . A strikingly original talent that deserves more widespread applause." —*London Free Press*

"For those who have ever pined for another in vain, this is a painful but amusing evocation of the dawning of humiliation, the death of hope, and the power of the human mind to over-analyze a relationship into oblivion." —*Financial Times* (London)

"Schoemperlen is the author of one of the best collections of short stories ever published in Canada. *At A Loss For Words* is as wry as her earlier fiction, and as subtly constructed as *Forms of Devotion* was innovative." —*Quill & Quire* .

Also by Diane Schoemperlen

Red Plaid Shirt
Our Lady of the Lost and Found
Forms of Devotion
In the Language of Love
The Man of My Dreams
Hockey Night in Canada and Other Stories
Frogs and Other Stories
Double Exposures

At A Loss For Words

DIANE
SCHOEMPERLEN

At A Loss
For Words

a novel

HARPER **PERENNIAL**

A Phyllis Bruce Book

A Phyllis Bruce Book, published by Harper Perennial, an imprint of HarperCollins Publishers Ltd.

Originally published in hardcover by HarperCollins Publishers Ltd: 2008
This Harper Perennial edition: 2009

Grateful acknowledgement is made to the following for
permission to reprint previously published material:

Grove/Atlantic, Inc: Excerpt from "Wild Geese" by Mary Oliver from *Dream Work*
by Mary Oliver, copyright © 1986 by Mary Oliver. Reprinted by permission of Grove/Atlantic, Inc.

HarperCollins Publishers Ltd: Excerpt from *Our Lady of the Lost and Found*
by Diane Schoemperlen, copyright © 2001 by Diane Schoemperlen.
Reprinted by permission of HarperCollins Publishers Ltd and the author.

House of Anansi Press Inc.: Excerpt from *Liar* by Lynn Crosbie, copyright © 2006 by Lynn Crosbie.
Reprinted by permission of House of Anansi and the author.

Lyrics from The Archive of Misheard Lyrics used by permission.
Access this website at: http://www.kissthisguy.com.

Riverhead Books: Excerpt from "Sam's Dad" from *Plan B: Further Thoughts on Faith* by
Anne Lamott, copyright © 2005 by Anne Lamott.
Reprinted by permission of Riverhead Books, an imprint of Penguin Group (USA) Inc.

HarperCollins books may be purchased for educational, business,
or sales promotional use through our Special Markets Department.

HarperCollins Publishers Ltd
2 Bloor Street East, 20th Floor
Toronto, Ontario, Canada
M4W 1A8

www.harpercollins.ca

Library and Archives Canada Cataloguing in Publication
information is available.

"A Phyllis Bruce book".
ISBN 978-1-55468-404-5

10 9 8 7 6 5 4 3 2 1

Printed and bound in the United States.

For my girlies
and for Dale

There is some truth to this, like all lies.
—Lynn Crosbie, *Liar*

I am a writer who cannot write. There are many reasons for this.

For starters, I didn't sleep well last night. In fact, I haven't slept well for many nights in a row. For weeks maybe, months even. I used to keep track of my sleepless nights, but now I've lost count. It was too depressing to continue logging one wretched night after another.

Perhaps I haven't had a good night's sleep in years. Perhaps I haven't had a good night's sleep in my entire adult life. Perhaps not even before that. When I was six, seven, eight years old, my mother used to give me Valium to make me sleep. Sometimes a whole tablet, sometimes just a half. I remember her at the kitchen counter at midnight, wearing the frilly yellow pajamas she called "baby dolls," trying to cut up the little blue pill (I remember them as blue, but maybe they were white, or maybe pink like the antidepressants I'm now taking) with my father's penknife, the one with a picture of a moose on the handle, the one he used to clean his fingernails after working in the garden or on the car. It was a tricky and frustrating procedure, this halving of the pill. I remember the sound the knife blade made when it finally cut through and hit the counter hard. Sometimes one or both halves flew out from under the blade, and then I had to crawl around on the kitchen floor until I found it: under the table, under the radiator, under the edge of the counter, or just lost in the swirly multicolored pattern of the worn linoleum.

"Mother's little helper," indeed.

Ever since then, I have longed for sleeping pills. None of the over-the-counter remedies have ever worked for me. They only make me even more wide-awake and restless than I already am. In fact, any medication that says *May cause drowsiness* on the label is guaranteed to make me increasingly jittery and anxious.

Two months ago, after much begging and whining, I was finally able to convince my doctor to write me a prescription. I loved those little white pills. They worked. But she would only give me a three-week supply, no refills. She is a very good doctor: cautious, conscientious, and thorough. I told her that a previous doctor once said he wouldn't give me sleeping pills because I have an "addictive personality." She said she had to agree with him. She grinned wryly. So did I.

And so I soldier on, sleepless, brought almost to tears by those idyllic television commercials in which attractive men and women drift off to sleep in luxurious bedrooms with immaculate bedding, fresh flowers on the bedside table, not a stray sock or undergarment anywhere in sight, while butterflies and stars float above their sweetly somnolent heads, in which, no doubt, visions of sugarplums dance. In the morning they are bright-eyed and bushy-tailed, eager to get up and get on with their exceedingly productive and purposeful lives. Clearly they aren't thinking, as I do each morning, How on earth am I ever going to get through this day?

Every night here: first I cannot fall asleep, then I cannot stay asleep, then I wake up too early and cannot get back to sleep. I used to be able to nap in the afternoon to compensate for nights like this, but now I can't even do that anymore.

I recently heard a sleep specialist interviewed on the radio, and she said there are at least seventy-five different kinds of sleep disorders. Some nights I think I have all of them.

A few weeks ago I read a newspaper article that said recent studies have proven that a person suffering from sleep deprivation can still perform routine mechanical tasks properly and efficiently, but that their ability to think and work creatively is severely impaired.

Well then . . . no wonder!

✍

I'm supposed to be thinking about the book I'm supposed to be writing . . . but I am thinking about you instead.

✍

It is July as I write this. It's hot, hazy, and humid, as summer increasingly tends to be in this part of the world. I'm worried about global warming.

I've always been very sensitive to the heat.

My fingers keep sliding off the keyboard in this heat. When I try writing by hand in my notebook instead, my pencil gets all slippery and my hand sticks to the paper. I cannot think in this heat. My head hurts in this heat. My glasses keep sliding down my nose in this heat. I get a prickly rash all over my body in this heat. All I can think about in this heat is this heat.

And outside in the yard, the flowers are all drooping, exhausted and limp. I really should go out there right now and give them a good long drink before they give up the struggle altogether and fall flat on their pretty little petaled faces.

Oh, how I wish it would rain.

☛

Four days in a row I've been unable to complete the crossword puzzle in the morning paper. I take this as a bad sign. Those unfilled little squares haunt me all day long. Sometimes I don't get the puzzle finished until bedtime, sometimes then only after a telephone consultation with my friend Kate, who does the same puzzle every day at her house on the outskirts of the city. But she is currently out of town, and I am on my own puzzle-wise.

Lately I cannot help but notice how many of the crossword clues and their eventual answers seem to be uncannily applicable to my current situation:

10 Across: Love intensely (5): ADORE

18 Down: Ponder morbidly (5): BROOD

15 Across: Self-centered (8): EGOISTIC

7 Down: Insincere (9): DECEITFUL

9 Across: Discarded (4-3): CAST-OFF

23 Across: Hard to pin down (7): ELUSIVE

19 Down: Easily manipulated (8): GULLIBLE

3 Across: Reject disdainfully (5): SPURN

21 Down: Betray trust (3): RAT

13 Down: Cowardly (9): SPINELESS

6 Across: Poisonous (5): TOXIC

1 Across: Like a bad dream (11): NIGHTMARISH

12 Down: Freed from captivity (9): LIBERATED

✒

At my age I should have known better than to get involved with you. At my age I *did* know better than to get involved with you.

But I did it anyway.

✒

I am thinking about how you said I could always trust you.

I was skeptical.

You said I *had* to trust you.

I wanted to believe you.

You *begged* me to trust you.

You were so earnest, so persuasive, so charming. So boyish and sincere.

I said I knew that if I could learn to trust you, it would make me a better person in so many ways.

You wrapped your arms around me.

I allowed myself to be convinced.

You begged me to trust you. And I did.

✒

For a week now, my refrigerator has been making a strange sound, somewhere between growling and gurgling, followed by a gulping noise, and then several minutes of silence before it starts up again. The refrigerator equivalent of sleep apnea, I suppose.

I know I should do something about this before it breaks down altogether. But I've been procrastinating. I really should call the repairman. He is very reliable and exceedingly prompt: he might well want to come over right away. He is also fastidious, allergic to dust, and (as I once discovered when he came to fix the dryer in the basement) afraid of spiderwebs. Which means that if I call him today, first I'll have to try and move the fridge so I can vacuum under and behind it before he arrives. And then I should also clean out its contents so he won't be offended by that bag of liquid lettuce, that bowl of fermenting strawberries, that blue-furred lump in plastic wrap that used to be a piece of pork and ham pâté (country style).

He is a brusquely pleasant middle-aged man named Ted, with tattoos, a long gray ponytail, and a silver ring in one ear. It seems safe to assume that he never imagined he would end up as a major appliance repairman. Much as I like Ted, maybe I should find a new repairman, one who is not so hard to please. I could just pick another one out of the Yellow Pages. There are at least two dozen listed, many of them with large ads featuring reassuring phrases like:

Prompt Friendly Service
Trouble Free Fast
Honesty Is Our Policy
Quality Repairs at Affordable Prices
38 Years of Experience
Family Owned and Operated Since 1969

But how can I possibly choose? This is repairman roulette. How can I know in advance what I'm getting? How can I know which ads are actually true? Isn't this how I ended up with Ted in the first place?

✍

At first it seemed ideal: you there in your city and me here in mine. I liked the idea of a long-distance relationship, having had so little success with those conducted up close. And it wasn't a *long* distance anyway. It was a short distance, with only a few hundred kilometers between us.

We agreed that we would see each other whenever we could. Of course, we were both very busy, but we would work it out. In the meantime, there were e-mails, many e-mails, daily at first, sometimes three or four a day.

Once you wrote to me seven times in one day!

And, of course, there were phone calls too, weekly at first, usually on Friday afternoon before we headed off to our respective weekends.

Once we talked for four hours straight!

You said, That was the longest phone call of my entire life!

I said, Me too!

At first it seemed ideal.

✍

For months now I've been obsessively reading books about how to overcome writer's block. There are more of these than the non-writerly person might imagine. They have lengthy and auspicious titles and subtitles like:

Room to Write: Daily Invitations to a Writer's Life

A Writer's Book of Days: A Spirited Companion and Lively Muse for the Writing Life

Unstuck: A Supportive and Practical Guide to Working Through Writer's Block

The Writer's Mentor: A Guide to Putting Passion on Paper

The Pocket Muse: Endless Inspiration: New Ideas for Writing

The Writer's Block: 786 Ideas to Jump-Start Your Imagination

The Midnight Disease: The Drive to Write, Writer's Block, and the Creative Brain

But so far I've found that these books share an unfortunate kinship with those over-the-counter sleep remedies: they are so full of promise and they may work for other people, but, so far, they do not work for me.

And yet I haven't given up on them. I'm still trying to follow their advice: *Don't panic. If you feel extremely anxious about writing, do some deep breathing before sitting down at your desk.*

Okay.

Yes, I am breathing deeply.

Yes.

I am.

Breathing.

Deeply.

Yes, I am breathing deeply.

After a few minutes, I find that all this deep breathing doesn't make me feel any more relaxed or inspired: it just makes me dizzy.

✍

I said, I have not had much tenderness in my life.

You said, I can fix that.

✍

I said, I've had too much heartbreak in my life. Over the years, I suppose I've become good at many things. But love is not one of them. I guess, on some level, I'm afraid of men. But I am *not* afraid of you.

I said, You make me feel utterly, totally, and completely safe.

I said, You are so kind. Which is the most important and attractive thing I can think of in a man. It has been my experience in life that many men are not kind.

I said, You are also sensitive, honorable, interesting, intelligent, enthusiastic, compassionate, charismatic, gentle, funny, honest, open, warm, and giving. Not to mention . . . extremely attractive in all ways!

I said, You are one in a million!

You said, I'm flattered by the way you see me.

✍

The writer's block books are cheerfully chock-full of ideas designed to help frustrated people break through the wall of wordlessness upon which they have been banging their hapless heads. Some of these are writing exercises: suggestions for topics, scenes, characters, dialogues, and descriptions. They are both abstract and concrete, large and small, serious and silly. They are like mysterious encrypted poems.

Write about hair.

Write about a river.

Write about a train.

Write about a sudden storm.

Write about the horizon.

Write about socks.

Write about a bed.

Write about a character who is losing control.

Write about a character who is suffering from writer's block.

Now why didn't I think of that?

✍

Write about the first (or last) person who broke your heart. If you had the opportunity to take revenge, would you?

What if the first and last person who broke your heart were one and the same person? What if the first time was almost thirty years ago, and then he blew back into your life without warning, and you thought, Now, finally *now* . . . now it is *my* turn to have a happy ending?

What if he said he had been working his way back to you for thirty years?

What if you thought this was the most romantic and seductive story in the world?

What if you thought being with him again would erase every rotten thing that had happened to you in the meantime: every heartbreak, every rejection, every betrayal, every disappointment, every minute of loneliness and despair you had suffered in the last thirty years?

What if you thought being with him again would make everything else make sense, because *this* was what you had been waiting for, *this* was what your whole life had been leading up to?

What if you thought *this* was your destiny finally arrived, your fate finally incarnate, this man finally returned to you after your thirty long years of wandering alone in the wilderness?

What if you thought *now* you were going to live happily ever after after all?

✍

I am thinking about the time you brought me a bouquet of lilies and a basket of blueberries from the market downtown.

I didn't have the heart to tell you that I don't like blueberries. In an e-mail afterwards, I told you they were delicious. But in truth, I left them in the fridge until they rotted, and then I threw them in the compost.

I did love the lilies though. (I'm not in agreement with my neighbor who once told me she doesn't like lilies because they remind her of funerals.) I put them in a clear glass vase and set them in the center of the kitchen table.

You were in my city for a business meeting later that afternoon, and you'd come to town early so we could have lunch together first. You'd be returning to your city directly after the meeting.

This was the first time you'd been to my house. I gave you the tour (small house, short tour). You dutifully admired every little thing, especially the floor-to-ceiling bookshelves in the living room, the kitchen floor which I'd retiled myself the month before, the bedroom which I'd repainted and redecorated the previous winter, and, of course, my study where I wrote every day and about which you exclaimed, I'm so honored to be actually standing here in the room where all your wonderful words are generated!

You marveled several times at how clean and tidy everything was. I assured you that I'd done a major cleaning in anticipation of your visit, but you said you didn't believe me. You said you were sure it was always this perfect. You were sadly mistaken but, harboring some long-standing issues with respect to my sketchy halfhearted housekeeping skills, I was secretly pleased.

The evening before, I'd prepared a large bowl of Greek barley salad and a chicken oven-baked in a special barbecue sauce according to one of my mother's favorite recipes. Once cooked, the chicken was best refrigerated overnight and then served cold. You said you remembered my mother making this once when you were at our house for supper thirty years ago. I doubted this, but I didn't say so. Again, I was secretly pleased to think that you would pretend to remember, even if you didn't.

It was such a lovely day that we decided to eat outside in the backyard.

We carried the salad, the chicken, and two large tumblers of cranberry juice out to the picnic table beside the maple trees. You suggested we have the blueberries for dessert, but instead I produced a bowl of cold shiny cherries already washed and ready to eat.

I was nervous having you there and didn't eat much, but you didn't seem to notice. You had two hefty helpings of chicken and salad. I took a picture of you there at the picnic table smiling and squinting into the sun.

Then we moved from the table to the lawn chairs in the shade of the black walnut tree. We ate the whole bowl of cherries, spitting the pits into the grass, and talking for two hours about anything that came to mind.

I was no longer nervous. The more we talked, the more it felt as if no time had passed since we'd been together thirty years ago. It was like picking up the conversation where we'd left off. Those two hours together again in my backyard seemed to last for all of five minutes, and then suddenly it was time for you to go off to your meeting.

After you left, I did the dishes and attempted to have a nap. I couldn't sleep. I couldn't stop thinking about you.

That night before I went to bed, I moved the lilies from the kitchen to my bedside table. Peach-colored and so fragrant, they perfumed the entire room. They lasted for more than a week. During that time, it seemed that I was able to sleep much better than usual. I told you I thought they must have magical soporific powers, that they were soothing me as I wandered through that frequently thorny place between waking and sleeping that we had talked about. (Yes, it seemed that you, too, were a career insomniac. Oh, we had so much in common!)

But then, just as they were bound to, the lilies began to die: single petals falling to the tabletop or slipping to the floor, dropping silently in the night, and each morning when I awoke, there were fewer and fewer petals left, until finally all that remained were headless stalks and crumpled leaves, which also then ended up in the compost with the blueberries.

I did not take this as a sign.

I knew it was simply the natural, ruthless order of things.

✍

Write about your favorite flower.
Write about your favorite fruit.
Write about your kitchen.
Write about lunch.
Write about bedrooms.
Write about what you see when your eyes are closed.
Write about what was left behind.
Write about what you are waiting for.
What am I waiting for now?

✍

The morning after we ate chicken and cherries in my backyard, I wrote you an e-mail in which I said, After you left, I could think of a hundred more things I wish we'd had time to talk about. But later I felt sad because I know it will probably be a long time before we have a chance to get together again. Alas.

I said, But thanks for such a wonderful day! There's just nothing better than spending time with you!

In your immediate reply, you said, What an amazing and incredible woman you are! I feel so humbled and privileged to have this connection with you. Life is complex enough, and relationships that are special and based on trust are so rare . . . ours is a gift that must be treasured. I have to confess, though, that the original attraction I felt for you is still there . . .

I said, Yes, it's still there for me too.

You said, It feels so very great to have this open and honest

exchange with you. A relief, in fact . . . for I realize now that I have
kept my true feelings inside.

⌐

You said I was an angel.
You said I was a treasure.
You said I was an inspiration.
You said I was a breath of fresh air.
You said, You are a gift to all of us who know you.
I said, I'm flattered by the way you see me.
At various times you said I was wonderful, beautiful, intelligent,
captivating, expressive, smart, remarkable, generous, genuine, tal-
ented, brilliant, wise, and patient.
I said, All the wonderful things you say to me make me feel like
a million bucks!
Sometimes you adored me in French, which, we agreed, isn't
called a "romance language" for nothing. You said, Tu est merveil-
leuse, magnifique, très très belle . . .
I, apparently, am a sucker for flattery.
How do you say that in French?

⌐

It's so noisy in the neighborhood this morning. It's very distracting.
The people next door on the left are having their bathroom
gutted and completely redone. I've been inside their house and I
know their bathroom is exactly like mine. Personally, I can't see
anything wrong with it. However . . . this costly and prolonged
project involves an industrious chorus of hammering, sawing,

15

and drilling, with faint radio music in the background. Their old toilet now sits in the middle of their front yard. The bathtub is in the back.

The people next door on the right are having the exterior of their house repainted. It used to be plain white stucco like mine . . . a little boring maybe, but I can't say as how I'm all that keen on the new color, which is a smudgy yellow with olive undertones. The painters are a jolly crew of shirtless muscular young men. There's much laughter and calling back and forth, much shouting along with the CD player they've set up on the front porch. All those rap songs sound the same to me: lots of swear words mixed in with the singer's pledges of undying love for God and his mama. Yesterday the young painters all had beer with their lunch.

There are also the crows, which have been squawking at each other since daybreak. If I had a gun, I would shoot them. Yes, I would. A murder of crows.

And now, to top it all off, here comes the street sweeper to make my morning complete.

Later in the day, no doubt, the rest of the neighbors will decide to mow their lawns, whip out their weed whackers, hammer a few nails, fire up their barbecues, have all their friends over, fill up the inflatable swimming pool for the kids, and play some loud music too. The fellow at the corner will probably get out his chainsaw to cut down that big branch that is hanging right over his garage.

Of course, I could close the windows against all this racket, but then I would die of heatstroke.

Of course, I could buy a small window air conditioner. And one of these days I will. My resistance to doing so before now is not based on environmental or economical objections, but rather on some chauvinistic pioneering notion that one should be tough enough to weather the heat without assistance.

✍

You said, I do not want to ever complicate your life. I can appreciate how unique this is, me coming back into the picture some thirty years later.

I would never want to upset the balance of your life.

I said, You haven't complicated my life. You've made me so very very happy.

You said, When you are happy . . . I feel happy too.

I said, I consider myself an unbelievably lucky woman to be loved by you. I am so grateful to have you back in my life. You will be forever in my heart.

You said, I echo your thoughts there. I am so very thankful for having been able to reconnect with you, and for us to have the time and opportunity to reveal our true feelings and emotions, and to give to each other the truest nature of who we really are.

Later: I said, Sometimes I wish I could just put you back in the box where I used to keep you. But I can't seem to manage it. I guess I'm going to have to cut off your legs to fit you back in there.

You said, What!!!

I said, Just kidding.

✍

You said, One of the aspects of a true and deep relationship like ours is that it all takes time . . . and communication. This is part of what makes it so rewarding, fascinating, complex, energizing, and terrific for the soul!

I said, Yes, you're so right.

You said, As challenges come before us, we will deal with them . . . together . . . . . as we have been doing each day, and will for all time . . .

I said, Yes, we will.

✍

Write about small injuries.
Write about a justifiable sin.
Write about a fragrance.
Write about the color blue.
Write about breasts.
Write about teeth.
Write about being underwater.
Write about the fault line.
Write about never and always.

✍

You said I was the one person in your life with whom you could always be open, honest, and revealing.

You said I was the last person on earth you would ever want to hurt.

You said I meant so much to you . . . so very much . . . and always would.

You said, I would never never *never* want to hurt you.

I said, If I didn't already love you so much, I would love you even more.

✍

Now I'm almost out of cigarettes. Only two left. This makes me very anxious. I can't concentrate. Yes, I know I've been smoking too much lately. Much too much. Yes, I know I should quit. Everybody who smokes knows that.

Yes, I will quit someday.

But not today.

Right now I have to make a quick trip to the corner store and buy another pack.

Right now.

✍

One day a few months back when I made my daily visit to the corner store to buy cigarettes and a Pepsi, I found a playing card in the parking lot, facedown on the asphalt. It was raining. Several cars had run over it. When I picked up the card and turned it over, lo and behold, it was the ace of hearts.

I took this as a sign: a good sign, an *excellent* sign. I took this as a sign that everything was going to work out right, a sign that in the end you would indeed come live with me and be my love.

I put the card in my wallet for safekeeping.

The very next day, when I went to Tim Hortons for my daily

iced cappuccino, I found myself waiting in line behind a young woman with neon pink hair who was nuzzling the tattooed neck of a young man with a shaved head and a pierced nose. He was carrying a large black shoulder bag. I didn't especially want to watch them kissing and cooing, so I kept my eyes down and concentrated on his bag instead. On it, there was a drawing of a gun in gold, a row of six red stick-on skulls, several Metallica decals, and, in the bottom right-hand corner, held in place by four large safety pins, a real playing card.

It was the ace of hearts.

Of course, I can see now that neither of these were signs. They were just playing cards, coincidentally the same.

Or if they were signs, they were *bad* signs.

Perhaps I should have paid more attention to the tire tracks on the first one, to the gun and the skulls on the young man's shoulder bag, and maybe also to the safety pins.

Or maybe if the cards had been the *queen* of hearts instead . . .

✍

In addition to the actual writing exercises, the writer's block books also offer dozens of prescriptive diversions intended to free a person's mind from the tyranny of trying to write and failing.

Writer's block, it seems, is like impotence (now politely called "erectile dysfunction" or "ED"). Performance anxiety: the more you worry about it, the worse it gets. In this way, writer's block is also, I realize, a lot like insomnia.

Instead of staring at your computer or your notebook with

hooded, drooping, bloodshot, bleary, and/or owlish eyes for hours on end, the books recommend doing something else for a while . . . in the hope, I presume, that the ability to write again will sneak up on you when you least expect it.

Take a bike ride.

I do not own a bicycle.

Bake a cake or a batch of cookies.

Too hot.

Go for a walk around the block.

Too hot.

Take a long shower.

I prefer baths.

Take a bubble bath.

Too hot.

Clean the bathroom.

Did that yesterday.

Mow the lawn.

Too hot. The grass is all brown and dying anyway, due to heat and lack of rain.

Lie on your back in the grass and stare at the clouds.

Grass too prickly. No clouds, just polluted haze.

Sit on the floor and build something with Lego.

No comment.

Visit a bookstore.

Much as I've always loved bookstores, lately, when faced with their banks of overloaded floor-to-ceiling wall-to-wall shelves, I cannot help but think that maybe there are already too many books in the world.

I am thinking about how, early on, I was always trying to find ways to entertain and amuse you.

On a frigid Monday morning in January, after a solid week of below-normal temperatures with record-setting windchills, I downloaded a photograph of a cruise ship and attached it to my e-mail.

I said, This morning I'm writing to you from my first-class cabin on this lovely little ship in the Caribbean. Soon we'll be docking in the Bahamas for a couple of days. But in the meantime, I'll either be in the spa enjoying the Jacuzzi, in the dining room savoring yet another gourmet meal, or out on the promenade deck admiring the ocean views . . .

Then I said, No, no, don't worry . . . I'm right here at home where I always am! But it doesn't hurt to dream . . . right?

You said, Dreaming is good . . . yes . . . a cruise would be divine. Someday we will do that together. Won't that be wonderful?

We also talked of going to Tuscany. Neither one of us had ever been to Europe but, judging by the prevailing stereotypes, we figured Tuscany must be the most romantic place in the world: those Tuscans were so passionate and hot-blooded . . . just like us.

I rented the DVD of *Under the Tuscan Sun* and watched it twice. After discovering her husband is having an affair, a thirtysomething writer played by Diane Lane divorces him and then succumbs to a crippling case of writer's block. She takes a trip to Tuscany at her friends' insistence. There she buys a decrepit villa from an ancient contessa who is at first reluctant to sell her the place, but then a pigeon poops on Diane Lane's head and the contessa changes her mind because this is a very good sign! Much construction and romance ensues. It all ends happily ever after for everyone.

I suggested that you rent this movie too, but you said you thought it would be too much for you: all that steamy romance.

Recently I watched this movie again (either because I liked it a lot or because I wanted to torture myself) and laughed out loud at a line I seem to have missed in my first two viewings: *What is it about love that makes us so stupid?*

I sent you the address of a website featuring Tuscan villas for rent, and I bought myself a Tuscany calendar that featured a small color photograph for each day.

There were statues and gargoyles, church domes and steeples, picturesque doorways, windows with blue shutters, endless fields of sunflowers.

A full moon floating in an inky Italian sky.

One perfect red hibiscus flower.

Clusters of blue grapes still on the vine, large toothed leaves in sun and shadow.

Dozens of loaves of bread packed on end in rough wooden shelves.

Rusted and battered metal signs: *Touring Club Italiano, Lampo Benzina Superiore, Trattoria Dell'Orso.*

Rows of tall narrow cypress trees, evenly spaced and pointy-topped, somehow ghostly-looking and eerie to North American eyes (the ones about which Sandra Oh in the movie says, "There's something strange about these trees . . . it's like they *know* . . . creepy Italian trees.")

Three hundred and sixty-five photographs and not a single person visible anywhere in any of them. Certainly not us.

✍

I am thinking about that time we were on the phone and you said you were making quiche for dinner, and I said, Mmmmm, delicious, I love quiche! (Thinking, Mmmmm, delicious, I love a man who can cook!)

You said you'd love to make quiche for me someday.

I said that would be heavenly.

(If, at the time, the old cliché "Real men don't eat quiche" crossed my mind, I don't remember it now.)

I remember that later that night I had an extended and detailed fantasy of you and me together in my kitchen, side by side at the counter, chopping green peppers and celery while something savory sizzled in the oven, and then you moved behind me and put your arms around my waist and pressed your front against my back and your lips against my neck, and then I turned gracefully into your embrace and we were kissing and swaying slowly to the music that had suddenly started playing softly out of the ceiling.

When I told you this fantasy the next morning, you said you'd been awake most of the night too, tossing and turning with your head full of similar dreams of our future together.

✍

I really should go to the grocery store. This too I've been procrastinating. At the moment, I'm fresh out of eggs, dish soap, bread, lettuce, laundry soap, orange juice, paper towels, baking soda, and oregano. Plus I'm running perilously low on cheese, bagels, vinegar, and toilet paper.

If I went right now, I could get one of those delicious frozen President's Choice Chicken Tortilla soups for lunch. They only take six minutes in the microwave. This is what currently passes for a home-cooked meal at my house.

(And what about dinner? What on earth am I going to have for dinner tonight? Maybe the President's Choice 100% Whole Wheat Rotini with Chicken Pesto or what about the Indian Lamb Rogan Josh? Really . . . it's much too hot to cook.)

To tell the truth, I've been avoiding the grocery store lately, mostly because of the music. While other such stores favor generic Muzak that renders all tunes nondescript and easily ignored, my grocery store plays real music. Whoever is in charge of the selection prefers vintage rock-and-roll and sappy love songs from the seventies. Sometimes this is fun, as on the day they were playing that old Ted Nugent song "Cat Scratch Fever," and men and women with hair like mine (that is, salt-and-pepper) were singing along and swaying their hips behind their grocery carts. But more often than not, the music makes me tearful. More often than not, it leads to sniveling in the cereal aisle, whimpering in the baked goods department, and, once, to downright sobbing in the produce section.

To tell the truth, between the heat and the heartbreak, I don't have much of an appetite anyway.

I haven't lost my appetite for coffee, however. I have to go and make another pot right now.

Yes, I know I've been drinking too much coffee lately. There's also my afternoon Tim Hortons iced cappuccino habit and too much Pepsi, which is my evening drink of choice.

Yes, I know this is a lot of caffeine. (Do you think this might have something to do with my insomnia?)

Yes, I know I should switch to decaf or herbal tea or to that very healthy, very green drink that my friend Kate likes, although even she says it looks like pond scum.

(Actually, I'm beginning to acquire a taste for this thick and complex concoction, which contains, among other things, apple, pineapple, lemon, and lime juices; mango, banana, and kiwi purées; broccoli, spinach, spirulina, barley grass, wheat grass, Jerusalem artichoke, and odorless garlic. I still find though that it's better swallowed with the eyes closed to avoid that "pond scum" effect.)

But right now I'm going to the kitchen to make another pot of coffee. Right now.

And while it brews, I might as well have another go at that damn puzzle.

What is an eight-letter word for "TENACIOUS"?

✍

Every time I open the fridge door to get milk for my coffee, I see the comic strip I've posted there at eye level with two ladybug magnets. In the first frame, a young woman sits on the couch reading a book. A young man stands at her feet with a basket full of folded clothes. He says, *All our laundry is now clean.* In the next frame, he says, *Of course that's only because I should be writing my novel and I'm procrastinating like mad.* In the final frame, she, from the couch, says, *Fridge needs cleaning,* and he says, *Ooooh. Good one.*

This has been on my fridge for so long now that it's all yellowed and brittle around the edges. The one beside it has been there even longer. This is a single frame, two women having coffee in a stylish restaurant. One woman says, *I want a man who's loyal, patient, honest, attentive, reliable, forgiving, unselfish, even-tempered, and a good listener.*

The other woman says, *You want a dog.*

✍

Naturally, all this coffee-drinking results in many trips to the bathroom, and every time I go in there, I'm reminded that I really should call the plumber. Despite all my best efforts and diligent employment of previously successful tricks and techniques, I still cannot get the bathroom sink unplugged. Entertaining though it is to watch the volcanic workings of baking soda and vinegar repeatedly poured into the drain, I think I need professional help.

I have no relationship with my plumber. This is nothing at all like what I have with Ted. I don't even know the plumber's name. In fact, the company whose services I use has many employees, and seldom have I had the same plumber twice. So it should be a simple enough matter to call and make an appointment. And yet I'm reluctant to give up the fight and admit that I've been defeated by what is likely nothing more than a recalcitrant ball of hair and toothpaste and soap. There is also the matter of having to pay someone fifty dollars or more to do something that will probably take all of five minutes.

So maybe I'll just keep trying.

Maybe I'll give it another go right now.

☛

After we first became reacquainted, we wrote e-mails back and forth every couple of weeks, getting caught up on all that had happened in our respective lives during the last thirty years or so.

Then you came to my house that day bearing blueberries and lilies, and we ate chicken and cherries and salad in my backyard. It was immediately after that that we found ourselves engaged in a lot of funny e-mail flirting, which seemed relatively harmless at the time.

Earlier, my friend Kate had referred to the progress of our relationship as "glacial," but after that visit it accelerated quickly.

I said, I wonder what would happen if we had just one kiss?

You said that having just one kiss would be like opening a bag of potato chips and having just one . . .

Then you wrote right back and said that probably wasn't the best analogy because you hadn't actually eaten a bag of chips in years, so maybe it would be better to say a bowl of cherries instead.

I said, Or a bowl of popcorn . . . or pistachios.

You said, I *love* pistachios!

I said, Did you know that pistachios originated in ancient times in the Holy Lands of the Middle East? It was common practice back then for lovers to meet in orchards on moonlit nights to hear the pistachios cracking open. This was considered a sign of good fortune and enhanced love. The Queen of Sheba claimed the country's entire crop for herself and her royal guests because she believed pistachios were the most powerful aphrodisiac.

You said, No! You made that up!

I said, No, I didn't! I read it in a magazine in the dentist's waiting room.

We talked a lot about pistachios as time went on. We talked about having a bushel of them, several bushels, a whole truckload of pistachios!

But now they're just one more thing in the grocery store that must be avoided.

Now when I'm in the mood for nuts, I buy almonds instead.

✍

It was May. I was here, you were there. In a lunchtime e-mail, you said, I've just been out for a walk. The tulips here are so beautiful! I almost wrote "two lips." Oops . . . . . . Freudian slip!

I said, Four lips are better than two! These two are going to have some lunch now . . . although they can think of a few other things they'd rather do!

You said, Smooch! Yes, I see what you mean . . . . . . four are much better than two!

I said, Thanks . . . I needed that! Not nearly enough smooching going on around here (i.e., zero!) to suit me.

You said, We are in total sync on that topic! Concentrating . . . . is very hard today . . . . (smiles).

I said, I'm thinking about pistachios . . . seven or eight hours' worth! There . . . now I've really done myself in! We've been very naughty today!

You said, Naughty . . . yes . . . I loved it! The sun shines more brilliantly now because of our shared thoughts. Gotta run . . .

Then off you went to a meeting, and I spent the rest of the afternoon washing my windows and dancing alone in the living room. I played U2's "Beautiful Day" six times in a row. I jumped around and sang at the top of my lungs until my windows were cleaner than clean.

✍

I read somewhere once that a cat's motto is "When in doubt, wash."

For writers, especially blocked writers, the motto must be "When in doubt, clean something, preferably your desk."

In the past week, I've reorganized my pens, my pencils, and my highlighters; my file folders, my envelopes, and my address labels; my extensive collection of Post-it Notes, my reams of blank paper (which I buy in many colors as I like to print my successive drafts in different colors), and all my many blank notebooks and journals (some of which I've had for years and never used because they are too pretty to write in).

Now I really should sort out my elastic bands. Although I never actually buy elastic bands, still I have enough to last me a lifetime, even if I live to be a hundred and fifty years old. Where do they all come from anyway? There is no need for anyone anywhere to possess so many elastic bands. I'll just take a few minutes here and throw away the stretched-out ones, the very old ones that have gone hard, the very small ones that I can never seem to find a use for. And while I'm at it, I might as well sort out my paper clips too. I really should throw away the rusty ones, the bent ones, the sprung ones that have lost their grip.

How much more time can I possibly kill with these simple organizational tasks?

The unflagging advance of modern technology has provided writers with a vast array of even more absorbing avoidance tactics. While sitting at the computer writing (or trying to write and failing to write), there is also always Solitaire to be played. My current stats are:

Games Won: 87

Games Lost: 884

Best Winning Streak: 2

Worst Losing Streak: 53

You have played Solitaire for 37 hours.

Surely another few games wouldn't hurt?

In addition to the ever-present distractions of Solitaire to be played and e-mail to be checked, I've also found it's entirely possible to spend whole days surfing the Internet, downloading new screensavers and wallpapers, rearranging or deleting old files, trying to figure out how to create a PDF document, changing the font on my current document and then changing it back again, checking grammar and spelling and number of words, renaming and otherwise managing my Web bookmarks, googling myself and my friends and long-lost relatives, downloading music and burning CDs, and scanning in photographs of my parents when they were young (also of a vacation to Minnesota we took when I was six and a farm machinery exhibit we went to when I was ten).

Yesterday I taught my computer to respond to spoken commands so that I can now tell it to "Quit this application" or "Move this to the Trash" and it will. I can also ask it to tell me a joke and it will respond with one of a seemingly unlimited repertoire of knock-knock jokes, delivered in any one of a variety of voices: male (Bruce, Fred, Junior, or Ralph), female (Agnes, Vicki, Kathy, or Princess), and novelty (Bubbles, Zarvox, Hysterical, or Deranged).

Knock knock.

Who's there?

Effervescent.

Effervescent who?

Effervescent for computers, I wouldn't be here.

All in all, the computer provides a blocked writer with many very satisfying and sometimes amusing diversions.

Gloria Steinem once said of writing that it was the only thing that, when she was doing it, she wasn't constantly thinking she should be doing something else. (I have just spent forty-five minutes searching for this quotation.) It is to this state of writerly nirvana that I aspire.

But these days it seems that writing (or trying to write and failing to write) is the only thing that, when I'm doing it, I'm constantly thinking of all the other things I should (or could) be doing instead. But that's not strictly true either. To make matters worse, when I'm doing most of those other things, I feel guilty and am

constantly thinking I should be writing (or trying to write and failing to write) instead.

In this lurching, peripatetic manner, nothing gets done.

✍

Watch a game show.
Take up yoga.
Wash the dishes.
Sweep the porch.
Play miniature golf.
Take some swings in a batting cage.
Treat yourself to a massage.
Attend a religious service.
Volunteer at a soup kitchen.
Make a salad with at least two ingredients you don't usually use.
Make a paper clip chain six feet long or more.
Go to an expensive restaurant by yourself.
Open an encyclopedia at random and read everything on that
page.
Resolve not to surf the Internet until you've written at least one
page.
Apologize to someone.

✍

You said it first.

It was about a month after you'd been to my house and we'd
had lunch together in my backyard. I was in your city on business,

doing some promotion for my new book. I'd taken the train up, and, courtesy of the publisher, I was staying at a majestic old hotel that resembled a castle with its limestone walls, its imposing turrets, and its regal soaring copper roof. We'd planned to have dinner at a much-acclaimed Moroccan restaurant just down the street. But it had been raining with a monsoon-like intensity all day.

It was only a short walk from your office to the hotel, but when you arrived, your shoes and socks were sopping wet. I could hear them squishing when you came into the room. You hung up your coat, took off your shoes, left them on the floor of the closet, and draped your dripping socks over the shower bar. Then you made liberal use of the hair dryer.

We reminisced about the last time we were together thirty years ago. It had been raining then too.

I said, We have a history with rain.

We decided to order dinner up from room service instead of going out. This seemed decadent and romantic, as befitted being ensconced in a castle that bore no resemblance to anything in either of our real lives.

Half an hour later a white-haired man in an immaculate black uniform wheeled a table into the room. It was covered with a heavy white linen cloth and in the middle sat a tiny crystal vase bearing three perfect purple stalks of freesia. He reached down into the warming cabinet and pulled out several dishes covered with shiny metal lids. He made a sweeping gesture toward the table like a game show host or a magician and said, Monsieur, Madame, votre dîner.

You tipped him generously. He went away and we arranged ourselves on either side of the little table. There was not enough room for your long legs, so we moved the dishes to the coffee table and sat side by side on the blue velvet love seat. For starters, we shared a large bowl of cold zucchini soup with basil and mint, and then a colorful parmigiano-topped salad of arugula, radicchio, and endive lightly dressed with a shallot-balsamic vinaigrette.

Then we started on our main courses. You had the poached salmon in saffron broth, with celery root purée and steamed asparagus. I had the chicken breast stuffed with asiago cheese and spinach, served with lemon rice. After so much soup and salad, I couldn't finish my chicken. You cleaned your plate and then mine too.

I said, I see you still love to eat!

You said, Yes, my appetite never fails me.

I too am usually a big eater (much to the chagrin of some of my friends, those who say they gain five pounds just looking at a piece of cheesecake). We agreed that we were lucky to have such high metabolisms that we could eat whatever we wanted and never gain weight.

Fortunately the desserts were small. I had the tiramisu and you had the raspberry torte. We fed each other tasty tidbits until both plates were empty.

Then you wheeled the table into the hallway. I put the vase of freesia on the bedside table.

Afterwards, we were curled up close on the love seat. It was still raining. We had been holding hands for hours. Time was passing so slowly that it didn't seem to be passing at all. For once, time was not flying. Instead, it seemed to have ground to a complete halt.

We had not kissed yet. We were not eating potato chips, cherries, popcorn, or pistachios. We were sharing a can of Pepsi from the minibar. (I gave up alcohol years ago. I said I didn't mind if you had a real drink, but you said no, you'd sooner share mine with me.) Your socks were still hanging in the bathroom. I'd taken my shoes off too, so we were both barefoot. I was resting my head on your chest.

You said, You smell so good. What's that perfume you're wearing?

I said, It's Obsession by Calvin Klein.

You said, He knows a thing or two about obsession, that Klein fellow!

We were both grinning. You were fondling and admiring my hair.

You said, I love your hair.

I said, I love *this*. (Meaning all of it: being there with you, quiet and close in the luxurious room with the lights dimmed and the rain still pounding outside and your heart pounding in my ear and the French classical music station playing on the bedside radio.)

You said, I love *you*.

I said, I love you too.

You said, Yes.

✍

I said, Over the years, my relationships with men have ranged from the ridiculous to the disastrous. I've often wondered if there was some lesson I should have learned from our relationship way back then that I didn't see at the time. Or something I *did* learn but then forgot. That scene of you driving away and me standing there in the rain sometimes strikes me as prophetic. There has since been a lot of driving away and a lot of standing in the rain. Sometimes I've been the one driving away and sometimes the one once again standing in the rain.

You said, I'm so sorry about what happened back then. I've always felt badly about the way things ended between us. At that point in time, I was a stupid young fool, naive and confused. I'm better now at communication than I was then.

You said, I made a mistake. I never should have left you.

I said, I never should have let you go.

You said, Now we've been given a second chance.

I said, Yes.

✑

I said, You must remember how much my parents loved you back then, possibly as much as I did. Especially my mother. Sometimes I thought she wanted you for herself! You're the only person I've ever been involved with that she approved of, before or since. I still can't get over the fact that she actually said she'd understand if I didn't come home that night, that last night before you left town, and after you dropped me off that rainy morning, she gave me coffee and Kleenex and let me stay in bed the rest of the day. I'm sure she's very happy right now! She's probably been up there in heaven lobbying God for years to bring us back together.

We were naked in the king-size hotel bed.

I said, I'll bet they're both smiling down on us right now.

You said, I hope they're smiling with their eyes closed!

37

✐

In the middle of the night, you got out of bed and tiptoed to the bathroom. Being a very uneasy sleeper and not accustomed to sharing a bed, of course I came instantly awake. Once my eyes adjusted to the darkness, I could see the crystal chandelier on the high ceiling of the hotel room. I heard the toilet flush, and then you made your way back across the room slowly and carefully in the darkness. You slipped back into the bed, naked and warm.

I said, Is this my life?

You snuggled in beside me. You said, I know I should leave you alone and let you sleep . . .

I said, No, don't.

I molded my body as tightly to yours as I could. I said, At home I have a book by Ellen Gilchrist called *I Cannot Get You Close Enough.* That's how I feel right now.

You said, Yes.

✐

In the morning I had to get up early to do a television interview. When I saw myself in the bathroom mirror, I shrieked.

I said, Look what you've done to my hair!

You said, It looks beautiful.

I said, So it's true then what they say: love really is blind!

My battery of hair products was spread across the bathroom vanity. You handed me the moisturizing mousse, the curling spray, the styling gel, the shine spray, one by one, solemnly, as if they were surgical instruments. Then you helped me scrunch my hair back into some semblance of a style.

I said, Nobody has ever helped me scrunch my hair before.

Then you sprayed a fine mist of the Obsession perfume at my throat and grinned lasciviously.

You wondered if I might have a razor with me, but I didn't. I did, however, let you use my toothbrush. You said you liked the taste of my toothpaste, a subtle citrus flavor with foaming action.

By this time your socks were dry so you put them back on, and then we went back into the room, me still naked and you in just your socks. I drew back the curtains and the sun came in. You stroked my bare shoulder, admiring the way the soft morning light shimmered on my skin.

Then you helped me get dressed. For the interview, I was wearing black dress pants and a black silk tank top with an elegant (and rather expensive) white linen overshirt. You held up the white shirt and I slipped my arms into the sleeves. You did up the pearl buttons and straightened my collar, rubbing the fabric between your fingers and commenting on its fineness.

I said, Nobody has ever helped me get dressed before.

You said, I'm just doing what comes naturally.

You helped me put on my bracelet. It had belonged to my mother, a souvenir my father had brought home for her over sixty years ago from the war in Holland. He was a radio operator in a tank. The bracelet consisted of nine Dutch ten-cent coins with Queen Wilhelmina on the front and the year 1941 on the back, soldered together with a series of intricate filigreed links. I held out my wrist and, with some difficulty, you did up the tiny tricky clasp. Your fingers were large and the blue veins in my wrist were pulsing. Your gentleness made me tearful. I had already told you how much it meant to me that you had known my parents when they were, if not young, at least both still alive and well, before my mother had cancer, before my father had Alzheimer's and no longer knew who I was.

I took the three stalks of purple freesia from the little vase on the bedside table, dried off their stems, wrapped them in Kleenex, pressed them carefully between several thicknesses of newspaper, and tucked them into my suitcase.

We stood in the doorway of the hotel room kissing for a long time before we left our castle. Before we walked back into the real world.

You said, This has been the most romantic and erotic night of my life.

I said, Me too.

You said, They really should put a historic plaque on the door of this room to commemorate the occasion!

I said, No matter what happens, we will always have this.

Write about rain.
Write about a doorway.
Write about a crystal chandelier.
Write about skin.
Write about the word desire.
Write about the word destiny.
Write about an argument between two people that begins in bed.

There was no argument.

At least not then.

At least not in bed.

✐

Write about the first encounter between two people who will eventually destroy each other.

Write about the first encounter between two people, one of whom will eventually be destroyed, while the other will go on with his life much as he always has.

(*Do not be so melodramatic. Do not resort to catastrophic language. Do not use the word* destroy.)

Write about the first encounter between two people who, after a time of great drama and intense distress, will both go on with their lives much as they always have.

✐

In a nod toward the time-honored notion of spring cleaning, I'd been looking through a box of old papers and notebooks in the basement. I found a diary I'd kept when I was only thirteen. From it, I sent you this quote: *I have always wanted to have a book written and published. I just don't know how many I've started but I haven't even finished one.*

I said, The grammar may be a little rough but the dream is clear. And I'm happy to say I've now finished a few!

You said that yes, you could concur that, from a very early age, writing was all I ever wanted to do. You said you remembered the very first conversation we ever had thirty years ago. I had to admit that I did not. We'd met in a bar where I shouldn't have been in the first place because I was underage. You said I'd told you then that I was going to be a writer someday.

You said, I remember you there, amidst the smoke and the crowd and the loud music, telling me with absolute clarity that this was what you wanted to do.

We were both young enough back then to be still making ardent declarations about what we wanted to be when we grew up.

Now you said, And here you are! A writer. A *great* writer! I am so impressed with all you have accomplished.

I said, I don't want you to be impressed. I just want you to love me.

You said, I do.

✍

When I first met you in that bar in my hometown thirty years ago, I was eighteen years old, in my last year of high school, still living in my parents' house, still a virgin. You were new in town, recently graduated from university elsewhere, hired to work in my city after applying for similar positions all over the country.

We danced together all night that first night and ignored everyone around us. Although I don't remember now what we talked about, I do remember that the band in the bar played a song called "Dancing in the Moonlight" and we declared it ours. In the following months, we went to that bar many times, usually with friends of mine from school or friends of yours from work. I remember that each night the last song the band played was "Brown Sugar" by the Rolling Stones.

We fell in love.

Although I'd been intensely infatuated with several boys who didn't know I was alive and had then progressed to much kissing and groping in cars with boys who *did* know I was alive but weren't much interested in talking or going steady for more than a week or two, still I'd never been in love before. I was entirely swept away.

You'd been in a long-term relationship before you came to my hometown. It had ended badly. You said you'd thought you were in love with her, but it was only now that you'd found me that you understood what love really was. We agreed that we had neither one of us ever felt this way before. (Now that I'm older and allegedly wiser, I know that people say this to each other every time they fall in love. Each new love cancels out all the old loves and each new love is the *best* love, rendering all previous loves delusional and counterfeit, sorry errors in judgment.)

We quickly became inseparable, always kissing, touching, whispering, gazing into each other's eyes while the rest of the world swirled on around us, unacknowledged and uninteresting.

You came to my house for supper every Sunday. My mother was not much of a cook, but you devoured every single thing she served and complimented her profusely on her culinary skills. No wonder she loved you so much.

My father loved you too. Every Sunday, he would move his tiny black-and-white television set from the bedroom to the kitchen and there the two of you would watch the hockey game after supper while my mother and I watched something else on the color television in the living room, a large brand-new console set that you called "the Cadillac."

43

When we weren't at my parents' house or the bar, we were in the room you were renting in a basement downtown. The bathroom was across the hall. There was a small black dog that was always looking in the window at us. There was something about oranges too: we were always eating and appreciating them.

Sometimes I helped you with your work, the two of us side by side (thigh by thigh) at your tiny kitchen table, you transcribing your notes while I did my homework or organized your index and your footnotes. It was hard to concentrate because we always had the music on and you were always rummaging in the fridge looking for a snack and the phone rang frequently and sometimes your friends dropped by with beer or burgers and your tidy single bed was always there, just five steps away on the other side of the room.

You were the one, the first one.

When you came back into my life, I had not had a date, let alone a romantic relationship, for more than ten years. I explained that this hadn't been for lack of opportunity. My celibacy was a choice I'd made, a decision to give up on love because I was so bad at it.

Laughing, I said, Not bad at the sex part, but abysmally bad at the romance part!

I said, I am a born-again virgin!

You said, Ten years?? With the knowledge that such a backlog of energy is stored up there inside of you . . . well! . . . I must say . . . . . images abound!!

And then you were the one . . . again.

I teased you about this afterwards. I said, What a truly remarkable man you are, taking my virginity twice in a lifetime!

I said, You were the first man I ever slept with, and now I hope you will also be the last.

Later: I realized this could play itself out in more than one way.

Still later: I sent you a paraphrase of a line from a novel called *Surrender, Dorothy* by Meg Wolitzer: *Sex leads to crying: this is a universal truth.*

✍

You said, I keep all your books on my bedside table. At night, when I can't sleep, I enjoy being able to open one of them at any page and read what you have written.

At the time, I said, It's very touching to know that you keep my books at your bedside . . . how sweet you are!

Now I say: Lately I find myself frequently opening one of my own books at random and reading what I wrote five, ten, or even fifteen years ago. I don't do this out of vanity. I do it out of the need to remind myself that yes, I am a writer. To reassure myself that yes, I've been doing this for years. Yes, I *do* know how to string a series of words together to form a sentence and then another sentence and another, to form a paragraph and then another paragraph and another and another, and the pages pile up, and sometimes it all turns out pretty well.

When I dip into my own earlier work like this, sometimes I discover that I was smarter then than I am now.

Now I say: If I may be so bold as to quote myself, here's a sentence I like: *It is only in retrospect that I understand that obsession has nothing to do with love and everything to do with anxiety, insecurity, uncertainty, and fear.*

I said, Several years before you came back into my life, I had an idea for a novel to be called *Beginning Middle End.* The story of a man and woman who fall in love when they're young and have a passionate romance, but it doesn't last (Beginning). They go on to live their separate lives (Middle). Much later they are reunited by accident. The last few sections would be alternate endings: happily ever after, unhappily ever after, ambiguously ever after (End). I cannot honestly say I consciously had you in mind when I made notes for this idea over ten years ago now . . . but the subconscious is always with us!

You said, Didn't most of the great writers of the last couple of centuries plunge headlong into the realm of romance? Great fiction has often been created from the tumult and, at times, the tragedy, of those writers' real lives.

I said, Yes, many great writers have been known to throw themselves on the mercy of their passions. So much great literature is about love, but why so seldom with a happy ending? All the tragedy that so often results from unleashed passion does indeed produce great literature, but not necessarily great lives. Personally, I prefer romantic comedies in which everything works out perfectly in the end! I'm longing for a happy ending myself . . .

You said, Me too.

I said, There seem to be a lot more happy endings in movies than there are in books. I've been watching so many romantic movies lately that I'm fairly swooning with the rapture of it all.

Maybe I should take up horror movies or action thrillers instead, just to give my poor heart a break!

You said, Last night I saw the most wonderful movie called *Before Sunset*. You really must see it. Their story is so much like ours. They were young lovers for just one night in Vienna, and then, ten years later (only ten years!), she shows up at a book signing he's having in Paris. I'll ruin it if I tell you more.

I said, Does it have a happy ending?

You said, I don't want to give away the ending.

I said, I won't watch it unless it has a happy ending!

You said, Yes, it does.

I said, Last night I did something I've never done before in my life . . . I painted my toenails red! The color is called Fever. My friend Michelle always has her toenails painted, so I decided to try it too. I'm so glad I did! Isn't it funny how sometimes a silly little thing can give such great pleasure? Every time I looked down at my feet today, I just had to grin. They do look very cute!

You said, I can literally picture your red toenails . . . and they look magnificent!

A couple of weeks later we were sending e-mails back and forth about my next visit. I was scheduled to do some more book promotion in your city.

I said, I'm counting the days.

You said, Me too. I've been missing you so much. I'll call the hotel and instruct the staff to have the rose petals ready . . . I'll tell them to strew them throughout the lobby to herald your arrival. I'll be waiting there with baited breath.

I did not say, If your breath is baited, you need to brush your teeth and break out the mouthwash. (I already knew you didn't always appreciate my sense of humor.)

I said, You are so romantic!

You said, When I see you again, I may just have to fall at your feet . . . and start kissing from there on up!

I said, Good idea! I'll wear the pretty red polish on my toes as it is very bewitching and sure to drive you crazy. (It isn't called Fever for no reason!) I'll also wear some of that Obsession perfume . . . and nothing else!

The following morning my computer would not cooperate. Before rushing it in for repairs, I managed to send you a quick note to warn you that I would be without my e-mail for a couple of days.

You said, Your poor computer! Perhaps that stunningly hot note you sent yesterday melted some microchips . . . or at least steamed them up a little??

When my computer was duly fixed and returned to its rightful position on my desk the following afternoon, of course I wrote to you immediately. I said, Oh, you are so smart . . . yes, the technician quickly determined that it was indeed that sizzling e-mail of Tuesday afternoon that caused my machine to melt down less than twelve hours later!

✍

I said it first.

I said, We are soul mates.

You said, I like that idea. Yes . . . soul mates . . . . . we always have been and always will be . . . . . I have always loved you . . . . and I always will.

I said, Yes.

✍

You said, You'd think that by this stage of my life, I'd be able to articulate my thoughts and emotions clearly and forthrightly!

I did not say, Yes, you would think so.

I said, You're doing just fine.

We were kissing at the time. In fact, we were kissing in an elevator at the time, an elevator in the building where I was going to do yet another interview about my new book. When we reached our floor and the doors opened, all the people waiting to get on grinned at us. I giggled, giddy with the excitement of both the kissing and the getting caught. You looked down at your shoes, but I could feel you smiling.

As we stepped out of the elevator, I slipped my arm through yours.

I said, I don't think I've ever kissed in an elevator before.

You said, Me neither. I feel like a teenager!

I said, Me too! (As if this were a good thing.)

You said, It's so gratifying to discover these feelings can be rekindled at any stage of life. I never would've believed I could feel this way again at my age!

I said, Me neither!

✍🏻

You said, I would do anything for you, my dear soul mate . . .

I said, I would do anything for you too. How can I tell you how much you mean to me? I hope you know.

You said, I am amazed at how in sync we are with our mutual feelings.

I said, We are so good for each other!

You said, Yes, we are!

I said, As my friend Kate would put it, you are the star in my firmament! (She is a brilliant poet, my dear Kate, so of course she has a way with words!)

✍🏻

After the first time we spent the night together (I mean the first time this time, not the first time thirty years ago), I came home on the train and immediately sat down at my desk and wrote you an e-mail. It was Friday evening.

I said, I hardly know where to begin. For once in my life, I don't know if I can find the words. Every moment of our time together was astonishing, amazing, incredible, heavenly, exquisite, miraculous, glorious, magical, rapturous, wondrous, unforgettable, and utterly divine.

I said, On my fridge I have a small magnetic calendar of fortune cookie sayings. Today's says, *Your first love has never forgotten you.*

I said, Do you know how happy I am? I'll be riding around on the love train here all weekend. I've got a silly grin stuck on my face and I'm always thinking, He loves me, he loves me!

I said, Do I adore you? Yes, I do!

I said, When I was there, you said you wanted to make me feel loved. Do I feel loved? Yes, I do! So very very much!

I said, Every night before I go to bed, I'll spray some Obsession perfume on my pillow so I can remember every single moment of being there with you.

After I wrote to you, I called my friends Kate and Michelle to tell them what had happened.

I said, He loves me, he loves me, he loves me!

Being all too familiar with my dismal relationship track record, they were cautiously delighted. They were both thrilled and worried at the same time. They said they didn't want me to get hurt again.

I knew they meant well but, determined to head off their ambivalence at the pass, I said, Please don't tell me to be careful. I *hate* it when people tell me to be careful. I'm a big girl and, for once in my life, I know exactly what I'm doing!

They said, We just want you to be happy.

I said, I know.

I said, I *am* happy.

The next day I mailed you one of the postcards I'd taken from the desk drawer in the hotel room. On the front a photograph of the hotel in springtime: turrets and chimneys, a hundred small windows in the limestone walls, copper roof gone green, the sky a deep cloudless blue, and beds of red and yellow tulips all around. On the back I said: *Once upon a time there was a fairy-tale castle. It was raining. The prince and the princess took shelter in a room with a blue velvet love seat and a crystal chandelier. All love and the meaning of life were revealed.*

I am thinking about the first time you told me you'd been sick with the flu, and I said I was so sorry I couldn't be there to take care of you. I said that, in my incarnation as nurse, I would offer cool cloths for your forehead, clear chicken broth, flat ginger ale, unsalted soda crackers, weak tea with or without honey, gentle temperature-taking, and frequent pillow-fluffing with fresh pillow-cases every hour on the hour. I said I would provide hand-holding, back-rubbing, and sponge-bathing as required.

Now I say: Oh please.

You said you were going away for a week because your cousin had died. He'd been killed in a car accident. The two of you had always been close. I said I was so sorry to hear of your loss. I said I was so sorry I couldn't go with you to help you through this difficult time.

I said, I'm going to miss you so much. I've grown accustomed to there being a certain number of miles between us. When that distance is greater than usual, I'm sadly and painfully and constantly aware of it.

I said, While you're away, I'll be sending you all my love and support in the old-fashioned way, without benefit of e-mail or telephone lines. So don't be surprised when suddenly you feel my hand in yours, my arms around your waist, gentle kisses on your neck, my head on your chest.

I signed this e-mail:
   Yours always,
   always yours,
   yours in all ways,
   me.
When I read this over now, it makes me squirm.

Now I say: Look what love does to language. Either it sends you straight into breathless, shameless, hyperbolic logorrhea (like then) or it leaves you wordless altogether (like later).

✍

I said, Yesterday we had thunderstorms off and on here all afternoon. Very odd for this time of year. I'm not usually fond of thunderstorms but, for some reason, this time I enjoyed them. Instead of feeling afraid, this time I felt they were something to revel in and marvel at. The tumult in the sky. So flamboyant and invigorating. At around 4:30, right in the middle of it, suddenly the sun came out, just setting low in the west. The sky became a peculiar and eerie combination of orange and gray and green that I've never seen before. The large red-brick apartment building I can see from my kitchen window was glowing an unearthly orange. When I went outside to have a better look, I discovered there was a double rainbow, two perfect semicircles stretching across the eastern sky. It was so beautiful that I got a little teary-eyed. I hope there was a rainbow at your house too. If not, you can have mine.

Now I say: Get your own damn rainbow.

✍

Write about an eclipse.
Write about an island.
Write about your reflection in a mirror.
Write about windows.
Write about bodies of water.
Write about borders.
Write about road maps.
Write about packing a suitcase.
Write about escape.
Write about the making of beds.
Write about then having to lie in them.

✍

I've just received a hilarious e-mail from my friend Michelle and now I have to send it to all my other female friends.

I used to check my e-mail fifty or sixty times a day. No, I'm not exaggerating. I was always hoping (endlessly relentlessly compulsively obsessively hoping) that your name would pop up perkily on my computer screen. I'm well past that now, but the e-mail is still there, and it still needs to be checked. Frequently.

There's always the spam that needs to be deleted, junk messages with jubilant exclamatory titles like:

This would look great on your wrist.
Look sophisticated on your vacation.
Melt away fat easily.
Become fit and happy again!

Make your fat friends envy you!
Have erections like steel!
My penis has gone from 3.5 to 6 inches and it's still growing!
Penis Enlarge Patch will make your dick so big you will be able
to park a car on it!

There are also those e-mails that consist of series of unconnected words that need to be puzzled over briefly before deleting:
*Cousin book thank. East given love purpose south. Taste mischie-
vous idea turn.*

Yesterday I received one of these called *frequent affluent atrium
cheese,* which contained over a thousand words strung together
without punctuation or capitalization. It began:

> *ethyl beautify deluxe creak melanoma baptism debarring acute
> anathema jeopardy romeo bomb gangplank amygdaloid errant
> digging quartz derriere concentric dictum horoscope annihi-
> late induce delusion accept indigestible mutton funeral hereof
> bittersweet bromine occidental finale fiendish pressure fahren-
> heit macrostructure quintessence herringbone auburn destitute
> creepy armadillo alizarin compost rampage paris goat . . .*

And it concluded:

> *. . . hibernate companion ballast bonnet prostrate hindsight pen-
> sion arcane expelled correspond simulcast combine improvisation
> accustom cypriot hecatomb epistemology polonium differentiate
> exponential heathen ferrous eyesore paraxial adjoin clasp gleam*

dextrose authenticate coven secede originate bounty pearl carci-noma repression bedspring marimba fanatic procrastinate rac-coon periphrastic fortify pocket hypnagogic paginate newsreel innocuous begrudge gloat shiny cripple roar

Just for fun, I printed this one out and it filled six whole pages, single-spaced. What is the purpose of these mysterious missives, I wonder? I suppose it's because I'm a writer that I find them so fascinating even though they make no sense at all.

But this morning's message from Michelle makes perfect sense to me. It's called *New Study*:

A recent study conducted by the Department of Psychiatry at UCLA reveals that the kind of man a woman finds attractive depends on where she is in her menstrual cycle. If she is ovulat-ing, she is most attracted to a man with rugged and masculine features. However, if she is menstruating or menopausal, she tends to prefer a man with scissors lodged in his temple and a bat jammed up his ass while he is on fire. Further studies in this area have been canceled.

Yes, I am menopausal.

✍

I said, Waking or sleeping, I dream of you.
This was not true then, and it's not true now.
At night I do not dream of you. Even when we were happy
(or some reasonable facsimile thereof, in those first few months),

56

even then I did not. Even at the height (or the depth) of my misery, I did not.

At night I dream of having sex in the backseat of a shiny red car with a large hairless man I've just met at a gas station on an empty highway bisecting a wind-blown desert that stretches from one horizon to the other, and afterwards I get out of the car and stand waving by the gas pumps as he toots his horn three times and drives away.

I dream that my neighbor's cat's tail has fallen off and is lying in my driveway, twitching but bloodless, as the cat stalks away, as imperious and unconcerned as ever.

I dream of bowling with a group of strangers all wearing short-sleeved blue satin shirts with their names embroidered on them, but the names are written in Chinese and I can't read them.

I dream that I've moved back into my parents' house and am sleeping again in my childhood bed, but it's much too small for me now and my legs are hanging off the end at the knees and I'm afraid that rats are going to eat my toes.

I dream that I'm married to a man named Leonardo who has red hair and only one leg, and he's making me a big batch of buttermilk pancakes for breakfast.

I dream of buying a form-fitting green silk dress and silver stilettos which I wear to a fancy party where I sit on a blue velvet love seat and drink a whole bottle of Scotch and still manage to talk intelligently to a man in a white tuxedo about stem-cell research. This man says he's come all the way from Venezuela to attend the party. I tell him that when I was in the eighth grade I did a geography project on Venezuela for which I received an A+. The man in the white tuxedo does not appear to be unduly impressed. This dream party takes place in a mansion as big as a hotel. There are glittering chandeliers everywhere, shiny marble floors, enormous oil paintings in elaborate gilt frames, and an apparently endless spiral staircase leading to the upper stories of the building. The staircase is filled with people. Every room is filled with people. The mansion is set on a hillside and the whole hillside is filled with people. At the bottom of the hill there is a river. There are people in the river too, their heads bobbing above the surface of the water like beach balls.

Many of my dreams are like this: crowded with people I don't know in places I don't recognize discussing topics I know nothing about. Sometimes these strangers know me even though I don't know them.

I think about you all day long, but at night I do not dream of you. I don't understand how this can be true. Perhaps there's a quota for how many thoughts you can have about any one person in a twenty-four-hour period. Perhaps if you exceed your limit during your waking hours, then you have to dream about something else instead.

You said, I think we are both people who deeply value honesty, trust, and loyalty.

I said, Yes, we are.

Or I said, I think we are both people who deeply value honesty, trust, and loyalty.

And you said, Yes, we are.

I cannot remember now who said what in this brief exchange.

✍

Write about the worst lie anyone has ever told you.

Write about the worst lie you have ever told anyone.

Write about all the lies you have believed even though you knew you shouldn't have.

Write about all the lies you've told so often and so well that you ended up believing them yourself.

✍

I said, Ever since we reconnected, I've sensed a certain sadness in you. Perhaps there is an answering sadness in me too. Maybe that's what soul mates are: the answers to all the questions we didn't know we were asking.

I said, My life hasn't worked out the way I thought it would. Although I'm proud of my various accomplishments, still they aren't enough to make a whole and happy life. Ever since I was a young woman, I've felt there was something missing in my life. Now I see that "something" was you! Now I see that I need love . . . I need *your* love.

You said, I do appreciate these thoughts. I want to say how much I welcome and treasure everything you say. Your letters are too wonderful! You lift my spirits immeasurably with all that you write. You warm me on this gray damp day.

✍

I said, Whenever I ask you how you are, you always say, "Fine." But sometimes I am not convinced. I know this question is usually a rhetorical cliché, but when I ask you how you are, I really do want to know the truth.

You said, When people ask me, "How are you?" I always say, "Fine." If they persist and say, "No, how are you *really?*" then I say, "Complex." Not to be trite about it . . . but this is how I see myself . . .

I said, Complex? Yes, you are! As I am discovering day by day, week by week, chapter by chapter, in this lifelong process of getting to know you. Not a bad thing at all . . . challenging sometimes, but always exciting! Complex, yes, also unpredictable. You certainly keep me on my toes! I think that I, on the other hand, am extremely predictable and not nearly so complex. You are inscrutable, I am transparent (or so I've been told many times). Kindred spirits and soul mates we are indeed, but very different in some ways. Opposites attract? A good balance? Whatever we are, I think we'll never be bored!

☞

You said, I try to be always in control of my emotions. I think we are so alike in regards to this . . . we always strive for stability of emotion in all aspects of our lives.

I said, Yes, you're quite right. My quest is for that often underrated (and recently elusive) middle ground between the ecstasy of the euphoric highs and the juggernaut of the desperate lows.

I did not say, Are you crazy? I have never striven for (nor attained) emotional stability in my entire life.

This morning the phone keeps ringing. It's so annoying. There have been six calls already. One to remind me of my dentist appointment next Tuesday, one to ask if I'm happy with my newspaper delivery, one wrong number for someone named Tiffany. The other three calls were just telemarketers. I don't answer these. I recognize their numbers in the call display. There's one who calls faithfully every morning between 9:30 and 9:45. I've often thought that if you were as reliable and predictable as this telemarketer, things would be different now.

My telephone has two different rings: a short one for local calls and a longer one for long distance. I'm ashamed to admit that sometimes still the sound of the long-distance ring gives me a jolt. I'm ashamed to admit that sometimes still I catch myself thinking it might be you.

Early on, I was always sending you horoscopes: yours, mine, ours. I usually prefaced these with the disclaimer that, of course, I didn't actually believe in them, but I read them in the paper every morning anyway (right before I started the crossword puzzle) just for fun.

MINE: The sun moves into the most dynamic and creative area of your chart today, so forget about all the things that have gone wrong in your life and look forward to all the things that will soon be going right. To say that big changes are on your horizon is an understatement. Anticipate something you could never have expected: things are bound to be exciting.

YOURS: Good news on the work front will get your week off to a great start, and it will get even better when the sun moves in your favor. You have worked extremely hard in recent weeks, and whatever it is that you are rewarded with today, you must not doubt that you deserve it.

MINE: Experiencing things intensely is par for the course for you, but right now the strength of your emotions, and how quickly they're changing, is incredible. There is no point in trying to stay calm. The best way to stave off depression is to have something to look forward to and, according to the planets, there are plenty of things in your immediate future that will put a big smile on your face.

YOURS: You'll be on the move a lot over the next few days, so make sure you are in the right frame of mind and in good shape physically. Also make sure you don't take silly risks while on the roads because there will be more than the usual number of crazy drivers out there. Stay cool, stay calm, and stay alive.

In the winter, your morning e-mails often began with a description of the commute from your home at one end of the city to your office at the other.

You said, I was late getting in today. I was held up on the grid-locked freeway.

You said, It's like a rodeo out there this morning.

You said, It's like a war zone out there today.

I said, We should compile a list of all the words we've used to describe your commute: grueling, onerous, tedious, frustrating, aggravating, exasperating, frightening, bizarre . . .

You said, It took me three times as long to get here this morning as it usually does. I'm exhausted before my day has even started.

I said, Oh, you poor thing.

And I meant it.

At the time, I used to check the Weather Channel every evening, and it would fill me with anxiety whenever the forecast for your city was bad. Freezing rain, heavy snow, high winds, whiteout conditions. Each morning after a forecast like that, I would hold my breath and pray for your safety until I saw your name pop up on my screen.

Later: When I watched the Weather Channel and they gave dire and alarming warnings for your city, I cheered.

Now: I figure the more weather adversity you have to face, the better.

✍

We were always saying that, given our relatively short amount of time here on earth, people must live in the moment, live *for* the moment. We were always agreeing about the need to live life to the fullest. We were well aware of the fact that we were not young anymore and did not have all the time in the world. *Carpe diem.*

We were always saying, Everything happens for a reason.
We were always saying, Nothing ever stays the same.
We were always saying, Life is short.
Life is *so* short.
Life is *too* short.

I said, Your eyes are so beautifully blue.
You said, Thank you.
I said, I cannot get enough of you . . . your words, your voice, your face, your smile, your skin, your strong arms around me.
You said, Now you're making me blush!
I said, Good.

I said, In my fantasy we are lying quietly together, naked, my head on your chest, or yours on mine. We are not talking. We are just breathing together. The room is slowly growing dark, the rest of the world is slipping silently away, and then we fall asleep in each other's arms.
You said, Now I'm weak at the knees!
I said, Good.

Write about euphoria.
Write about light.
Write about shadows.
Write about fireworks.

Write about sirens.
Write about circling the edge.
Write about falling from grace.
Write about loneliness.
Write about yearning.
Write about the elephant in the room.
Write about betrayal.

✍

Early on, I used to send you the addresses for websites I thought you'd find interesting or amusing. Sometimes I sent you these because I couldn't think of anything else to write about except "us," and I didn't want you to think I couldn't think of anything else to write about except "us."

Knowing how much you loved the outdoors, I sent you the address for the Sound Archive of the British Library, which features recordings of all manner of bird songs, including those of the African Hoopoe, the Algerian Nuthatch, the Burmese Bushlark, the Hispanic Coal Tit, the Fiery-Necked Nightjar, the Lemon-Rumped Warbler, and the Slate-Colored Boubou. There are animal sounds too: the Baboon, the Badger, the Koala Bear, the Edible Dormouse, wolves howling, cattle mooing, horses whinnying, pigs grunting and snorting. You could even listen to the sounds of an approaching thunderstorm or of pinecones splitting open in the heat. You'd often said how cooped up you felt when you had to work in the office all week, so I thought you could listen to these sounds throughout the day and feel better.

I sent you the address for a foundation called Save the Mustangs, dedicated to saving wild horses. I knew you cared passionately about this endeavor. The website included the story of a woman named Janet Burts who had successfully removed more than a hundred horses from Canadian pregnant mare urine farms to safety in Alaska. (I didn't mention that I knew about PMU farms and how the urine of pregnant mares is used in making birth control pills and estrogen replacement drugs because my cousin's husband and his brother used to own a PMU in Manitoba. I didn't mention that, for their efforts, the brothers were excommunicated from the Mennonite Church. Back then, the problem with PMUs was about the birth control pills, not the cruelty to animals. I didn't mention that, after a time, the brothers gave up the pregnant mares and raised buffalo instead. This was back when trendy restaurants were serving buffalo burgers for the novelty of it.)

I sent you the address for the Archive of Misheard Lyrics. Everyone loves these. I knew you would too. For example, I wrote, in that classic Rolling Stones song, "Beast of Burden," the first line has been variously misheard as *I'll never be your big Suburban . . . I'll never be your Easter bunny . . . I'll never be your big stuffed bird . . . I'll never be your bacon burger . . . I'll never leave your pizza burnin'.*

And in the Robert Palmer song, "Addicted to Love," the lyric from the chorus has been most frequently misheard as *You might as well face it, you're a dickhead in love.*

✍

Thirty years ago, like all young (and not-so-young) couples, we had our own special song: "Dancing in the Moonlight" by King

Harvest. A short-lived American band of the seventies, they were a one-hit wonder with this tune, singing about how getting it on most every night was a supernatural delight, and we don't bark and we don't bite, we like our fun and we never fight, you can't dance and stay uptight, we keep things loose and we keep things light.

Between the time you left me behind when I was eighteen and the time you walked back into my life almost thirty years later, I don't remember ever once hearing this song. But after you reappeared, I heard it everywhere: on the oldies radio station, in taxicabs, in shopping malls, in the grocery store. Once in a movie soundtrack and again on a television show.

Once I heard it in a department store where I was contemplating buying a shirt. I was holding the shirt up in front of myself in the mirror, admiring the tiny rhinestones on the front and the lettering that said *Les Environs de Moulin 1913 . . . Palais des Beaux Arts . . . Mise en Musique par M. L'abbé Dugué,* but wondering if its predominantly beige color made me look washed out. Then the song came on in the store.

Of course I took this as a sign.

Of course I bought the shirt.

Of course I wore it the next time I saw you.

Of course you loved it.

I discovered on the Internet that the old album including this song is now available on CD, so I ordered two copies, one for each of us. I mailed yours with a card that featured a photograph of a luminous full moon reflected in a gelatinous body of black gleaming water, and it said, *When I am moon-gazing here . . . I love knowing that you are seeing the same moon there.*

I added my own words at the bottom: *Still and forever dancing in the moonlight with you. Love from me.*

You said, I am so touched by your gift and your words. Thank you with all my heart. I love the moon and I love you too.

✍

Write about the moon.

I already have.

I'd been reading a book called *Moonscapes: A Celebration of Lunar Astronomy, Magic, Legend, and Lore* by Rosemary Ellen Guiley. I said, You know my astrological sign is the moon sign. I should be an aficionado on the subject!

I sent you a list of Native American lunar names from the book:

Moon of Frost on the Tepee
Moon When the Little Lizard's Tail Freezes Off
Limbs of Trees Broken by Snow Moon
Raccoon's Rutting Season Moon
Ripening Strawberries Moon
Moon When Horses Get Fat
Spider Web on the Ground at Dawn Moon
Every Buck Loses His Horns Moon
Hunger Moon
Sap Moon
Fish Moon
Worm Moon
Milk Moon

Wart Moon
Rotten Moon
Honey Moon
Moon with No Name

You said, Thank you so much for sharing these. They are so beautiful and poetic, as are you. I will never again look at the moon without thinking of you, oh my Lady of the Many Moons.

✍

Thirty years ago, you left me behind to take a job elsewhere, a better job two thousand miles away. At the time, I thought my broken heart would never heal.

I still have the four letters you wrote to me after you left. For all these years, I've kept them in a battered wooden cigar box that once belonged to my father, who never smoked cigars.

Our correspondence back then was conducted long before the advent of e-mail, and so your old letters were handwritten on flimsy lined foolscap with an untrustworthy pen that blotted frequently. I have them still in their original envelopes. Back then, postage was only eight cents.

I've read these letters over many times in recent months.

The first one was written three weeks after you left me standing in the rain in front of my parents' house. I'd passed those weeks in a welter of misery. I went to school every day because my mother made me, but once there, I spent an inordinate amount of time in the girls' bathroom smoking and fixing my mascara after crying on the shoulders of all my friends. I was the first of my group to lose her virginity, and after you left, I found that my friends were every bit as fascinated by and obsessed with my abandonment as they'd been with my initial deflowering.

In those weeks, I pretended to do my homework in the evenings, but really I was in my bedroom crying, hiding from my parents, listening to sad music, and wishing I were dead. In those weeks, I (former straight-A student) failed an algebra test, got caught skipping English class twice, was late handing in a history essay, and then got only a D on it.

In those weeks, I swore that I would never fall in love again, that I would live the rest of my life alone, solitary, and sad, loving you forever and ever, and never looking at another man ever again.

Your first letter began: *That had to be the saddest goodbye I have ever spoken. The early morning, the rain, the tiredness, and thoughts of my long trip ahead . . . they all combined to shock me into realizing that the great time we had spent together was really over. You gave me some beautiful moments and much happiness in that time, and unfortunately the price paid was a lot of pain at the end. I hope I gave you enough good feelings, for I certainly wanted you to feel appreciated.*

It was a long letter, five single-spaced pages. The rest of it was about your trip, the weather, the price of gas, the sights you saw, the hitchhikers you picked up along the way, one who was going all the way to the east coast and another one, younger, a teenager who seemed to be running away from home.

As I remember it now, once I had your new mailing address, I wrote to you every day.

Your next letter didn't arrive until a month and a half later. It began: *Howdy there. I should have written earlier. There is no excuse. If you haven't done it already, I deserve to be cursed to the fullest.*

You said, *The last month here has been really really hectic. This new job is incredible. It's been a steep learning curve. They keep pressing us for reports and stuff . . .*

You said, *It is that tied-down feeling I am trying to overcome. I just feel like rambling all over this world. I think I will.*

You said, *Please accept this letter as a peace offering. Once I get settled down, I'm going to get better as far as writing to you goes. Thank you for writing despite my failure to reply. They were neat pieces of writing . . .*

Your next letter was written only three days later. As I recall now, these two actually arrived on the same day. This one was filled with details of all that you were required to do in your new job, also anecdotes about the many new friends you were making and all the wild parties you'd been to. I remember being impatient with all of this and skimming quickly to the end of the letter where I thought there would be something about love, something about the future, something about *me*. But there wasn't. I wanted pages and pages of lovey-dovey stuff, but instead I got all these stories that had nothing to do with me, and then, in closing, you said it was late, almost 1:00 AM, well past your bedtime and you had better turn in now. In a P.S. you asked me to please say hello to my parents for you.

Shortly after this I graduated from high school and also celebrated my nineteenth birthday.

Shortly after that I started going out with someone else.

I was young, after all, and had the attention span of a gnat. I wrote and told you about my new romance. Upon receiving this news, you were supposed to come roaring back to my hometown and claim me for your own. I wanted you to come galloping back on your white charger and wrest me away from him and keep me all for yourself forever and ever amen.

(I realize now that these fantasies may have been a bit Neanderthal, certainly not feminist, in nature, and might well have involved you dragging me away from him by the hair. In my own defense, I can only say that I was desperate, I was young, I wanted *passion*, I wanted *drama*.)

What I got was one more letter from you, one more letter that didn't arrive until four months later. For six whole pages, you told me about encountering a bear while you were out camping in the bush, about seeing a car on fire while driving back from a party, about the various projects you were working on, about the many interesting people you were meeting, and about a used car you were thinking of buying.

Then, at the very end of this long and detailed letter, you wrote, *I'm pretty darned happy for you and your newfound love. You'll both be good for each other, I can tell. Undoubtably, he is one lucky guy, due to the fact that he is going out with you. I will never forget you. I think (when I take time to do so . . .) that I will always see you in a romantic light. I would like to keep in touch, as long as I am not a burden to you.*

I did not hear from you again for almost thirty years.

I did not see you again until the day I was giving a reading at a small bookstore in my old hometown and you were the first person to walk through the door.

I shrieked in a most unbecoming way and cried, I know you!

Although I hadn't laid eyes on you for thirty years, I would have known you anywhere. It appeared that we were both aging well.

We hugged hello. You said you were in town for a couple of days to visit an old friend who was having heart surgery that afternoon. You said you'd read the notice of my reading in the local newspaper the night before.

At the time, we marveled at what a coincidence it was that we would end up back in my hometown at the same time after all these years.

At the time, my legs were shaking.

Later: We said it was fate.

Later: You said if it hadn't happened then, it would have happened in some other way because we were meant to be together in the end.

That day you couldn't stay for the reading because you had to go to the hospital. But you gave me a beautiful card. A hand-painted landscape of lake and trees and hills on the front and inside you'd written: *So proud and privileged to have known you in the days when you had hopes and dreams of becoming a writer. Now you are one of the best ever . . . . Much success and happiness for you in the future . . . .*

You said it would be nice to keep in touch now that we'd found each other again. I agreed and gave you my card with my e-mail address on it. I was so rattled I didn't think to ask for yours.

Back home again a few days later, telling Kate and Michelle

about your unexpected appearance at my reading, I was surprised to discover that I'd never told them much about you. I filled them in on everything that had happened between us thirty years ago. But I did my best to downplay the intensity of emotion I'd felt when you walked into that bookstore and hugged me hello. I did not want to admit (not then, not even to them, perhaps not even to myself) how thrilled I was to see you again. I was so used to being disappointed that I was afraid even to hope I'd actually hear from you again. This sort of thing did not happen to me.

If Kate and Michelle, who knew me so well, suspected there might be something more to this innocent little story of an old boyfriend showing up to say hello than I was letting on, if they could just imagine how far ahead I'd already leapt with this story in my head, they didn't say so.

For two weeks I checked my e-mail obsessively, but there was nothing. It appeared that I was right: actually hearing from you again had been too much to hope for. I tried to stop thinking about you. I succeeded fairly well.

Two weeks later, a month then since I'd seen you, you sent me a long and emotional e-mail reliving our time together thirty years ago.

You said, I will always remember that rainy morning when I last saw you . . . dropping you off at your parents' home. I truly drove all that night with a very heavy heart.

You said, I don't mean to intrude so profoundly upon you with all these old memories. I guess they have always been there but never expressed. I think now that's why I came to see you at that book signing a month ago . . . to thank you for the times we shared those many years ago. And simply to see you again.

You said, You saved me in so many ways. You restored my faith in love, women, and myself. If I'd had more sense way back then, I would have stayed with you.

I was so surprised and astounded by your outpouring that I didn't reply right away.

A week later you wrote to me again.

You said, I am concerned that with my note a while back I may have overstepped the boundary between just sending along greetings and bringing forth painful elements from a time years ago. I do apologize if anything I wrote gave you cause for exasperation. It was great to see you and I wish you all the best . . .

I wrote back within the hour.

I said, It's taken me a few days to answer your first letter because I was quite blown away by all those memories. And I just didn't know what I wanted to say. I still don't really, but here I am.

I said, Your thoughts about the past made me feel all weepy. It was so long ago. And so very sad for me in the end. But I have never had any bad feelings toward you because of what happened. We were both so young, me especially. I do think about it sometimes. I was so in love with you and I just couldn't understand why we couldn't be together forever.

I said, I'm happy that our paths have crossed once again. I look forward to learning more about your life. I'd love to hear from you again soon.

And so it began.

✍

My mailman has just been and gone, leaving nothing of note in the box for me. Phone bill, water bill, Visa bill with a joyful congratulatory note informing me that, due to my excellent handling of my account, my credit limit has been increased. Invitation to a Super Carpet Liquidation Sale (*2 DAYS ONLY! Over $3,000,000 of the finest Hand-Knotted Authentic Persian and Oriental Carpets from various BANKRUPTCIES are offered to you at GREAT SAVINGS*). Catalogs from L.L. Bean and Victoria's Secret. I have never bought anything from either of these stores and probably never will.

A month ago when I went to check the mail, the doorknob came off in my hand. I took this as a sign. I stood there staring down at the round brass ball in my right hand and thought of you, how this meant I would never hear from you now. The broken doorknob somehow forced me to admit to myself that, having not heard from you for so long by either e-mail or phone, still there was a small sad part of me that was secretly hoping you might be in touch with me the old-fashioned way. A small foolish part of me that was secretly hoping you would send me a letter, a *real* letter, not an e-mail, a real letter on good stationery in that handwriting I would recognize anywhere. A real letter that would explain everything, so that I would finally be able to understand exactly what had happened between us and why.

The broken doorknob somehow forced me to realize that this was what I was waiting for. I was still believing that you had all the answers and that eventually you would give them to me.

76

Now my front door can only be opened from the inside by means of a delicate maneuver with a pair of pliers. Sometimes it takes five or six tries to get the door open.

I really should go to the hardware store and buy a new doorknob. And while I'm there, I should also check out their small window air conditioners.

Do I have any idea how to install either a new doorknob or a window air conditioner?

No, I do not.

☞

When I asked if you still had the letters I'd written to you thirty years ago, you said they'd been lost in a move shortly afterwards.

You said, I have always regretted this . . . so very much.

I was disappointed, but I did find some notes I'd written in my journal in those excruciating weeks immediately following your departure.

Among many other rhapsodic, sappy, and embarrassing things, I had written, *I remember the night I asked you if you believed in premonitions. When you said yes, I knew I could tell you mine. My words came from the depths of my existence and I believe in them—blindly, perhaps, but unquestioningly. That night I said that I really couldn't believe it would be the end when you left. I said I knew that someday you would come back to me and we would be together as one once again.*

I wrote, *Now I hear a strange sound outside my window. Can it be pigeons cooing? No, it must be doves on a foreign horizon. A* sign: *peace and love are coming back to me. I can feel an inner calmness emanating through me as I write these lines, fill these pages. I feel loving and giving. I pray that it lasts.*

Apparently it did not.

✍

These days I allow myself to check my e-mail only every thirty minutes. I've just received one from someone named Desirée. Never in my life have I known anyone named Desirée. The subject line is *Whatever.*

Her tall round-shaped expensive gun calms down. Whose white silver mouse shows its value the time that our children's soft green table adheres. Her daughter's expensive carpet lies. The white t-shirt falls. A given golden carpet is thinking. The smart gun adheres. Our green golden eraser looks around. Mine purple round house is thinking. Her brother's fancy car is angry as soon as their silver white book fails. His small magazine lies. Our round-shaped sofa is angry and perhaps their red bed is thinking.

What, oh what, oh what does it mean? Is it a secret message written in a code accessible only to the initiated? Or maybe this Desirée person is also suffering from writer's block and has been reading the same books I have. Maybe this is her response to one of the writing exercises: *Write random words. Just type without stopping. Write any words that come to mind without trying to make sense.*

✐

I am thinking about how unfortunate it is that your first name is so popular and so common. It would've been much easier for me in the aftermath if your name were Aloysius or Cornelius, Engelbert or Elmo.

But as it is, I hear your name everywhere.

On the radio: announcers, musicians, interviewers, interviewees, they all share your name.

On the television in both commercials and programs: a buffoonish but charming husband who's always getting himself into silly escapades and trying to play tricks on his wife in a way that makes me think of him as a male Lucille Ball; an FBI agent not-so-secretly in love with his partner and the sexual tension between them is palpable, but you know they'll never actually get together because it would ruin the whole show; a rugged-looking man touting the best new denture cleaner, the best new car, the best new refrigerator, the best new antidepressant, or the best new erectile dysfunction medication.

Once a man who shared your name was a five-time champion on *Jeopardy!*, and for a whole week I had to listen to Alex Trebek saying his name over and over again with growing enthusiasm as he racked up the dollars, before eventually being bested by a grim-faced woman in a black-and-red striped turtleneck that vibrated on the screen.

On a downtown street, I hear one man calling out your name to another across the way.

In the checkout line at the grocery store, the cellphone of the woman in front of me rings and when she answers, it's someone with the same name as you, and she is overjoyed to hear from him, saying your name over and over and over again, a dozen times in a three-minute conversation.

One of the men who installed my new furnace had your name too, embroidered in red on a little white patch on the left breast of his blue coveralls. I'm sure he wondered why I kept staring at his chest.

For a while, it seemed that every novel I read included a character with your name: sometimes he was the hero and sometimes he was the villain. Sometimes he was just a minor character: dog walker, next-door neighbor, waiter, store clerk, ex-husband, nasty little boy, demented grandfather, a horse (once), and a dog (twice).

At first, every time I heard or read your name, my stomach would do a happy skipping loop and I would grin like a silly goose. Later, every time I heard or read it, my stomach went into a knot and I could not catch my breath. Once or twice, on an especially bad day, my chin began to quiver and my eyes filled with tears.

Now when I come across your name, I can only sigh and roll my eyes.

One of these days I'll come across your name, and it will be just an ordinary name, one shared by millions of other men (and animals), a popular and common name that is nothing special to me.

One of these days I'll go to bed at night without thinking of you.

One of these days I'll wake up in the morning without thinking of you.

One of these days I'll go all day long without thinking of you, and I won't even notice that I haven't.

✍

Many times I've googled you, and I've found that, in addition to your usual self, you are also an evangelical pastor who writes hymns and other sacred songs, a bookseller specializing in fantasy fiction, a collector of Civil War firearms, the owner of an asphalt company, the owner of an antique store, the vice president of a communications corporation, a risk analysis consultant, a jazz saxophonist, a forensic accountant, a disc jockey, a filmmaker, a Web designer, an oncologist, a psychiatrist, a criminal lawyer, and a high school football coach. You are also a street in Seattle, a road in Wyoming, a hiking trail in Oregon, a lake in New Mexico, and a mountain in Alaska.

Complex?

Indeed.

One in a million?

I guess not.

✍

You said, I love to hear the sound of the train whistle off in the distance . . . it always makes me think of you . . . of the train bringing you to me.

At this point we had not actually seen each other for four months.

I said, You are so romantic. I love trains too, always have, and now yes, at night with the windows open here, I can hear the whistles too, and I always think of you. A haunting sound, filled with a potent mixture of joy and melancholy, happiness and longing. On a clear night I can even hear the wheels humming on the silver rails.

I did not say, When I hear the train, me here alone in my bed, wide-awake in the middle of the night as usual, I put my fingers in my ears and the pillow over my head. Sometimes I also hum.

Later: I said, These past few weeks have been an utter train wreck for me.

Apparently the irony of this was lost on you.

✍

Chronicle the longest amount of time you have ever gone without sleeping.

Chronicle the longest amount of time you have ever gone without sex.

Chronicle the longest amount of time you have ever gone without love.

✍

You said, It's going to be another one of those weeks . . . I'll be out of the office every day, plus I have to attend three evening meetings in the outlying areas! So I will be charging around the region again. Did you know that last year I drove close to 80,000 kilometers?

I said, Good God! Did you know that the circumference of the earth is 40,076 kilometers? This means that last year you drove around the world twice!

✍

You said, I was only away for three days, but when I got in this morning, my voice mailbox was full and locked, and there were 183 e-mails waiting for me!

I said, Only six of them were from me!

You said, I will have to knuckle down here and get caught up on these. I only have two hours to do so and then I have to attend a meeting on the other side of town.

I said, You are an amazing man who will indeed be able to complete in just two hours what would take anybody else all day!

I said, I admire your dedication to your work.

✍

Perhaps I should have paid more attention to the fact that, while my newspaper horoscopes were almost always about love and romance and high emotion, yours were almost always about work.

YOURS: This may be an unsettling time in your career, but it is also a time of great opportunity, so keep your eyes and ears open, and keep telling yourself that you were born to succeed. If you say it often enough, you will start to believe it, and if you start to believe it, strange and beneficial coincidences will begin to occur.

MINE: Yours is one of the most emotional signs of the zodiac, and today's aspect between Venus, planet of affection, and Jupiter, planet of excess, will exaggerate your feelings, both good and bad. Try not to go over the top in what you say and do today, because it is likely to cause you some embarrassment later on.

YOURS: If you are not exactly sure what is expected of you at work today, don't be afraid to ask a few questions. It is better that others think you are a little slow than that you plow ahead without really knowing what you're doing and make a serious mistake that will have tremendous repercussions later on.

MINE: As Venus moves into the most dynamic area of your chart today, you will find you can persuade almost anyone to do almost anything. Don't waste this precious gift: use it to get whatever, and whomever, you most deeply desire.

YOURS: Your work colleagues seem to think you will do anything they ask of you. It's true that you like to be helpful, but if your work gets to be too much for you today, you must call a halt. You'll be no good to anyone if you do too much and have some kind of breakdown.

✍

When not actually at my computer sending you an e-mail, I was always writing to you in my head. Every day I was looking for things to write to you about the next morning.

I wanted you to know I was fine, just fine, busy, always busy, going on about my business with pleasure and enthusiasm. I wanted you to think I was a strong and independent woman having a full and happy life without you.

Sometimes this was actually true.

But not always.

I didn't want you to know that sometimes I was just moping and mooning around all evening, sprawled on the couch in front of the television in my housecoat before eight o'clock, clicking through the channels like a robot, eating coffee-flavored Häagen-Dazs right out of the container with my hair in an uproar and my eyes blurry with unshed tears, occasionally scribbling notes in the margins of the *TV Guide* of things to write to you the next day: too lazy in my malaise, too tired from my emotional exertions, too paralyzed by my own wretchedness to get off the couch, walk across the room, and get a proper piece of paper.

I didn't want you to think I was miserable . . . at least not all the time.

Early on you once said, I find it so totally rewarding and gratifying to learn about all that you are doing, thinking, and observing!

So I told you about art show openings, poetry readings, book launches, choir concerts, plays, and movies I'd been to.

I told you about the books I was reading and sent you quotes I thought you would enjoy. Sometimes, if I especially loved a particular book, I'd buy another copy and mail it to you. For these, you thanked me profusely. You said you now had a special bookshelf just for my books and these others I had given you.

You said, I never have as much time to read as I would like . . . but don't you worry . . . . I promise I will get to all of them eventually!

Frequently my e-mails began with a weather commentary. Our cities were in close enough proximity that we were sometimes suffering through the same weather systems. So then we could commiserate.

In the fall I complained about the endless raking of leaves, the need to turn the furnace on already, and the increasingly early darkness.

I said, Why do the days seem to get shorter so much more quickly in the fall than they get longer in the spring . . . inquiring minds want to know!

In the winter I told you about shoveling snow (over and over again!) and how it was so cold here that my back door had been frozen shut for four days in a row. I said, Let's call this "The Winter That Wouldn't Die"!

On a glorious Monday morning in mid-April, I said, After complaining about the weather all winter, I guess today it would be only fair to give Mother Nature her due and sing her praises. I worked outside all weekend cleaning up the yard, and I also found a little time to sit in a lawn chair with my feet up and my eyes closed. The feel of the sun on your face at this time of the year is so particularly wonderful!

Through the spring and early summer I told you about gardening, planting, pruning, and the joys of mulching, which I had just discovered. I told you that an infestation of white grubs had almost totally destroyed my front lawn, and then the rest had been dug up by rodents searching for those fat tasty grubs. I had to reseed the whole thing.

As the summer wore on, I complained repeatedly about the heat, the humidity, and the lack of rain.

I said, I'll be so glad when summer ends. Let's call this "The Long Hot Summer from Hell"!

You said, I love summer so much and I always get so melancholy when it ends. I try and hang on to the feeling of this season for as long as possible.

I said, Last night I succumbed to the heat and the temptation of summer sloth. I spent the entire evening sitting out in the backyard, eating a whole pint of Häagen-Dazs and reading the latest issue of *Glamour* magazine, which is filled with important and instructive articles like "10 Beauty Mistakes Everyone Makes," "How to Find Your Body's Perfect Jeans," "The Importance of Doing . . . Nothing," and "Men's 99 Unspoken Sex Secrets: The Man Manual Every Woman Should Read."

You said, They are forecasting a break in this heat wave tomorrow. Hopefully some relief from the high temperatures and the humidity will be more conducive to your writing.

I told you about finding a giant moth attached to the back wall of my house, laying eggs on the stucco. I got out my insect book and identified it as a Cecropia moth. I downloaded a picture from the Internet and sent it to you, along with the following information: *In northern climates the Cecropia moth emerges from its cocoon in late May or early June. Late at night, the female emits a scent called a pheromone that attracts the males. With his sensitive antennae, the male can find a female from over a mile away.*

I said, Wow . . . isn't that impressive?!

You said, It is indeed a rare pleasure to see these moths. I've seen one only twice in my life so far, once when I was just a boy and then again about ten years ago.

Apparently you did not want to discuss the sex life of moths.

I told you about helping my neighbor make a photo collage for her friend's seventieth birthday. I told you about my other neighbor cleaning out my eavestrough for only twenty dollars! I told you about yet another neighbor who was celebrating her ninetieth birthday. For the occasion, her daughter had hired a bagpiper who came down the street in full regalia, his kilt and sporran swinging while he played "Scotland the Brave," and everyone up and down the block came out of their houses and cheered him on. I told you how, although I have only a smidgen of Scottish blood in my ancestry, as always the sound of the bagpipes made my heart swell and my eyes fill with tears.

I told you about playing a vigorous and rousing game of Ping-Pong with my friend Kate. I said, Now there's a sport I really like! Besides all the shrieking and leaping about, what I especially like is the sound the ball makes when it hits the table. Do you like Ping-Pong?

I told you about going out for Chinese food with Kate and Michelle and some of our other friends, and after ample helpings of sweet and sour chicken balls, ginger onion beef, and almond guy ding, my fortune cookie said, *You never show your vulnerability. You are always confident and self-assured.* (I said, Ha!) After dinner, we all went bowling. Having not bowled since I was a kid, I was definitely the weakest player of the group, but I enjoyed myself anyway and the others tolerated my clumsy ineptitude with good humor. I asked you if you liked bowling, but you didn't answer.

I told you about having lunch every Friday with Kate and Michelle, usually at Kate's house, often in her big backyard if the weather was good, and how sometimes we went for a long rambling walk afterwards and how much we all enjoyed this. I told you about what we ate and what music we listened to and what books and movies we talked about. I didn't mention how much we also talked about you.

I told you about having my new furnace installed, and one of the workmen had the same name as you. I told you that the bathroom sink was clogged up again. I told you about my electrician not charging me for installing a new ceiling fan in the kitchen and asking for a signed copy of one of my books as payment instead. I told you about one of my kitchen cupboard doors falling off because of a broken hinge and how then I couldn't find a replacement hinge that would fit. I told you about the city workers' strike going on here and how my garden shed was full of stinky garbage and my laundry room was overflowing with recyclables, but the good thing about the strike was that parking all over the city was free! I told you about eating President's Choice Multigrain Alphabet Pretzels, spelling out your name and then gobbling it up with glee. I told you about seeing a fox calmly crossing a six-lane thoroughfare in rush-hour traffic right in front of a convent and how everyone stopped and patiently waited while he made his way to the other side. I had never seen a fox in the city before. I told you I thought it must be a sign, a sign from God, a sign from you too, of course, and that made me very happy.

I told you about hitting a huge pothole so hard driving home from a choir concert on a blustery rainy night that the rim of the front passenger-side tire was bent and I had to take it in for repairs. You said your car was in for repairs that day too: a broken fan belt. Two days later I told you that my toilet needed to be replaced and the plumber would be coming to do the job tomorrow morning. You said you were having plumbing problems that day too: a pipe in the basement had sprung a leak in the night and the plumber would be coming this afternoon.

The following Tuesday you called and I missed it because I was putting out the garbage, lugging two heavy bags to the curb for collection the next morning. I called you right back. You said your garbage day was Wednesday too!

I said, Isn't it amazing that we had car repairs on the same day and then plumbing problems too! And now it turns out that our garbage is collected on the same day! Coincidence? I think not!

When you're in love, there is no such thing as mere coincidence. Every little thing becomes weighty with meaning and significance. Even the trivial domestic exigencies of car repairs, plumbing emergencies, and garbage collection become fodder for further proof of your miraculous and unshakable psychic connection.

When you're in love, every little thing furnishes further evidence of the fact that the two of you are indeed fated to live together happily ever after. Amen.

✍

All the writer's block books advocate varying your normal writing habits and routines as a possible way of breaking through your current impasse. They are especially keen on the idea of writing elsewhere, anywhere other than at your desk.

Write in a diner.
Write in a deli.

Write in a coffee shop.

Write in a laundromat.

Write in a bus depot.

Write in a train station.

Write in an airport.

Write in a church.

Write in a cemetery.

Write in a park with children playing all around.

Write in the woods while leaning against a tree.

Write in the dentist's waiting room.

Write in the backseat of your car.

Write in bed.

Write in your pajamas.

Write in the nude.

Write while standing on your head.

I told you about an evening when I went out for dinner with my friends Lorraine and John, a long-married couple I've known for almost twenty years. It was a beautiful late August night. We sat on the courtyard patio of a popular downtown restaurant. I told you I had the sautéed lamb loin, not because I'm so keen on lamb (I do like it, but while eating it, must not think about the curly little fellows frolicking in fragrant meadows), but because it was done in a Middle Eastern style with an unusual salad of Israeli couscous and *pistachios!* I said, So of course I had to have it, and it was delicious!

After dinner there was music, a local group playing a variety of medieval songs in different languages, with violin, cello, mandolin, bass viol, and even a hurdy-gurdy. I told you I loved the music. I told you I had a fabulous time.

In truth, I've never been fond of medieval music, and I was sad all evening long because you weren't there with us. Even Lorraine and John said how nice it would have been if we were a foursome.

In my e-mail the next morning, I said, What made the evening so enjoyable was thinking how much you would have enjoyed it too, and knowing that I'd be telling you all about it today.

I said, No matter what I'm doing, I'm always wishing I was doing it with you.

✍

Write about a time you were misunderstood.

Write about a time you lost something important.

Write about a time you didn't say something that should have been said.

Write about a time you said something that shouldn't have been said.

Write about a time you said yes.

Write about a time you said no.

Write about a time you got what you wanted.

Write about a time you didn't.

✍

I am thinking about how, early on in this, I told Kate that I wanted to share every little thing with you all the time, and I didn't understand this insatiable need I now had to tell you *everything*:

every thought that crossed my mind, every meal I ate, every boring and mundane thing I did in a day (from cleaning the oven after having not done so for two years to getting my hair cut to having my teeth cleaned to washing down the bathroom from ceiling to floor and every surface in between). Sometimes it was as if my life had become a story I was telling you, as if I were now living in a novel or a movie and narrating every movement I made for you and only you, my singular and spellbound audience.

To Kate, I said, Sometimes this drives me crazy. Why is this happening? What's wrong with me?

And Kate said, gently, That's just the nature of love: it makes you want to share your whole self with your loved one.

I thought she must be right. In all that I told you, I was wanting you to *see* me, to *hear* me, to really *know* me for who I really am.

I am thinking about how later, after another week of roller-coaster ups and downs, I told Michelle that all of this was making me feel sucky and weird. I said, Sometimes this drives me crazy. Why is this happening? What's wrong with me?

And Michelle said, not unkindly, That's just the nature of love: it makes you feel all sucky and weird.

I thought she must be wrong. At least I hoped she was.

Now I think they were both right, my wise friends Kate and Michelle.

✍

In an e-mail written immediately after one of our marathon phone calls, I said, I love the way we talk! I love the way we're both so eager to speak that sometimes we're even talking over each other! I'm sure we'll never run out of interesting things to share and discuss . . . I truly feel that we can say anything to each other . . . this is so special and rare.

I said, It felt so good to laugh with you today. I think of you as a very calm person who is able to take things as they come. When I'm feeling rattled and alarmed and overwhelmed, just the sound of your sweet voice helps me get my balance back!

I said, Sometimes it still surprises me how important our connection is to my overall sense of well-being and happiness. When we are able to communicate, I feel so uplifted and recharged. I can't think of anything I enjoy as much as talking to you . . . okay, well, yes, maybe I can think of a couple of other things!

I said, I am *besotted*. (Now there's a delightful word that doesn't get used nearly often enough!) If I were there, I'd track you down wherever you were and give you hugs and kisses every hour on the hour! You are my heart's desire.

I said, Let me love you forever. Let me take care of you and make you happy. Forever.

You said, Yes, it was so wonderful to hear your voice, your thoughts, your ideas. What a precious thing we have! I so much appreciate your canny intuition. You are so good at coaxing my true feelings out of me. You are right that I have typically held back from sharing my emotions, and so this is a big departure for me and I appreciate it so much. The times I have been able to do this in the past are far and few between. I treasure the fact that we have this strong connection, and feelings for each other that transcend distance and time and that have lasted throughout the full extent of our adult lives. I do so very much appreciate having the privilege of what we share . . . . in all its forms . . . . . ups downs sideways . . . etc. You have made my day, my night . . . . and as time goes forward, my life . . . so much better . . . . . so much happier. Thank you.

Later: I said, Isn't it ironic that early on, we talked so often about how well we communicated? We were always congratulating ourselves on being able to talk so easily about anything and everything. But now you cannot find even five or ten minutes to give me a quick call or send me a note. I cannot help but think that if you really wanted to be in touch with me, you would be.

You said, Things are coming down to the wire here . . . my days are now predominately locked into tending to the work at hand . . .

I am thinking about how at first you said I was so wonderfully inquisitive, always asking questions, and how this was such an endearing and fascinating quality.

Later: You stopped answering my questions, even the trivial ones about bowling, Ping-Pong, television, or what you had for lunch today.

I complained about this, jokingly at first.

You said, I will indeed try and get to the questions you've raised, but it may take me most of the week, to be honest. I am working furiously to meet some deadlines here today and tomorrow . . .

When I began to complain with growing aggravation and ill-disguised anger, you said, In regards to responding to your questions . . . . . I want to do this very much . . . I have not had time . . . . my boss is on holidays and I am holding down the fort . . . . . I am not ignoring you or avoiding anything . . . nor will I.

☙

Draw with sidewalk chalk in front of your house.
Cut shapes out of construction paper.
Get up and dance.
Plant some flowers.
Have a nap.
Change your clothes.
Shave your head.
Light a candle.
Say a prayer.
Have another nap.

☙

You said you wanted to protect me.

I said, I do not want to be protected. Not from you anyway.

At the time, much as I protested against it, I found your desire to protect me rather endearing.

Later: I found it aggravating and, eventually, insulting. I felt that you were treating me like a child who could not be expected to cope with reality.

Now I think: The person you most wanted to protect was yourself.

✍

As things became increasingly difficult for me, on the advice of my friend Lorraine, I bought a book called *Reinventing Your Life: The Breakthrough Program to End Negative Behavior . . . And Feel Great Again* by Jeffrey E. Young and Janet S. Klosko. It is an interesting book that helps readers identify their own lifelong self-destructive patterns and then offers a variety of techniques to help change them. The book calls these negative behaviors "lifetraps."

According to the book, I most definitely have abandonment issues. It also seemed probable that, in addition to the Abandonment ("Please don't leave me!") Lifetrap, I might also be suffering from the Emotional Deprivation ("I will never get the love I need!") Lifetrap, the Defectiveness ("I am not good enough!") Lifetrap, and the Vulnerability ("Catastrophe is about to strike!") Lifetrap. This was a lot of lifetraps to think about all at once, so I decided to focus on abandonment for starters.

At the time I was reading this book, you were extremely bewildered by the problems I was having with anxiety and insecurity. I'd already told you that I'd never had much luck with love and romance.

I said, This insecurity of mine is a wild beast that comes out of my past bad experiences in the love department, a nasty old demon that I thought I had conquered.

I said, There's really nothing you have said or done that has caused this. I generated it all on my own, and it has to do with my own issues, my feeling that I am not lovable.

You did not seem to want to explore my insecurity any further.

It seemed that you wanted to talk about other things: basketball, the Olympics, a horse you owned when you were a teenager, a funny e-mail you'd received from one of your colleagues.

But, me being me, with my obsessive need to be understood (and my equally obsessive fear of being *mis*understood), I couldn't stop trying to explain myself and my own apparently puzzling behavior.

I said, I don't know what comes over me sometimes . . . a frisson of . . . je ne sais quoi! I think I need more time before I'll actually be able to believe this isn't all just a dream. I mean, really . . . you . . . me . . . together again after all these years? Sometimes it seems so unbelievable, too good to be true. Sometimes I think I must have made it all up!

I told you about this book that Lorraine had recommended.

I said, I think the book is right: I think I have abandonment issues.

You said, Abandonment issues? Well, *everybody* has those!

At the time, I laughed and said, Yes, of course, you're right!

Now I say: What the book doesn't address is that, often enough, when a person suffering from the Abandonment Lifetrap is afraid she's going to be abandoned, it is not necessarily a set of inappropriate feelings triggered by something innocuous and welling up from past bad experiences. Often enough, when a person suffering from the Abandonment Lifetrap is afraid she's going to be abandoned, she is right.

✍

We were in a room at the luxury hotel once again. It was not the same room. Although I'd requested the same room when I made the reservation, they said they were unable to guarantee any specific room. So we were in a different room, same floor, across the hall, several doors down. This room, less expensive, was much smaller and less elegant than the other one. It overlooked the noisy street rather than the pretty courtyard. There was no chandelier this time, just a smoke detector on the ceiling with a tiny red light that blinked continuously. No blue velvet love seat, just two small armchairs on either side of a small round table. I chose not to take any of this as a sign.

You'd said you would be there at one o'clock. You didn't show up until five to three. For those two hours I had paced around the room talking to myself, crying intermittently, drinking Pepsi from the minibar, and smoking many many cigarettes while standing by the open window because I knew you would not appreciate the smell of smoke in the room if and when you eventually arrived. I obsessively watched the traffic below, searching for your car. I checked both the room phone and my cellphone a dozen times to be sure they were working. I called both Kate and Michelle but neither of them were home. I imagined that they were out somewhere together without me and I cried a bit with home-sickness. I thought about calling Lorraine but decided against it, seeing as how she was the one who had most often warned me to be careful.

When you finally got there, you apologized profusely and said you'd been delayed due to yet another meeting, called without warning right after lunch, and it had dragged on and on and inter-minably on, and you had not been able to call me and let me know you would be late.

By the time you arrived, I was having a full-scale meltdown. In fact, this was the first time I'd allowed myself to break down in front of you. You brought me Kleenex. You took the plush white hotel bathrobe off the hook on the bathroom door and wrapped it around me although I was still fully clothed. I stepped into your arms. We lay down on the bed. You held me for a long time. We did not make love.

A few hours later I had to go home.

In my e-mail of the next morning, I said, It's never hard for me to tell you how much I love you and how much you mean to me. But it was *so very* difficult to let down all my defenses like that and tell you how truly messed up I've been feeling. Your being late was more than I could bear on top of everything else. I'm still a bit shaky. I didn't want it to be like this . . . I wanted it to be soft and lovely. I wanted to be always wise and smart and all those wonderful things you've said about me.

I said, You were so right when you observed that I love order . . . also reliability, predictability, and routine. All these things make me feel safe and in control. For so many years I've stayed away from men because I was afraid of being hurt again. It is only because it was *you* that I allowed myself to take a chance and let my guard down again. I thought you would never hurt me.

I said, For so many years I lived behind a wall, and right now I want to put that wall back up again. Right now I feel like my life has been thrown into total chaos and that is very frightening and upsetting for me.

I said, Having now told you how bad I've been feeling, I worry that you'll think less of me. I feel that everything has changed between us and our relationship has shifted yet again. Now you see a side of me that isn't incredible and amazing and wonderful. Now you see that I too can be weak and needy and unable to cope on my own. This really bothers me!

You said, I actually think more of you now, rather than less. In revealing the depth of your worries and emotions, you have become more real to me.

You said, It is certainly natural that we suffer with a myriad of feelings and emotions that go up, down, and all around. Life sure is complex at times. But also highly interesting, challenging, and, hopefully, as positive as it can be. I think the best way to proceed is to honestly put forth our concerns and always talk things out together.

You said, Please don't put that wall back up again.

I said, Although I've had some bad days recently, mostly I feel so very thankful for all of this love (*your* love!) that has come into my life at a time when I believed I would never feel love or be loved again. And so my dear soul mate, despite the difficulties, I have to say: I wouldn't have missed it for the world!

I said, I know I'll never be the same again . . . and I'm glad!

Your e-mails were always speckled with ellipses: sometimes the standard three dots . . . sometimes four, five, six, seven. At first I thought they were charming, your dot dot dots. When I told you this, you were a little embarrassed.

You said, I confess that when I first started writing to you, I was very self-conscious about everything I wrote, the spelling, the grammar, the structure, the punctuation . . . because you are such an amazing writer. All of your letters are of publishable quality, you know! They are always so perfectly wonderful. Writing to you has improved my confidence about my own writing skills, which is something I have always worried about. When I was in university my essays always came back covered with red circles and arrows pointing out my grammatical mistakes. And even now, with all the reports I have to write, I still have problems this way.

You said, When I use those dots, it makes me feel more like we're literally having a real conversation.

I said, Please don't be embarrassed or self-conscious. I love your dots! In them, there is breathing, sighing, thinking, smiling, laughing, teasing, stuttering, longing, hand-holding, hugging, sometimes just taking a drink of coffee, sometimes unshed tears, sometimes kissing, sometimes composing your thoughts or yourself . . . those dots are very versatile! Those dots are a punctuation revolution! So please don't hold back . . . send me your thoughts . . . send me your dots!

I even started using them quite often myself . . . those dots were like a spotted contagion between us.

But later: They were maddening. I would stare and stare and stare at them, as if they were a kind of hieroglyphics or Morse code that I would be able to decipher eventually if only I tried hard enough. But trying to read between the dots was even more exasperating than trying to read between the lines, even

more impossible than trying to make sense of those e-mails from
strangers that are just long nonsensical lists of unconnected
words. I would peer and peer and peer at your dots, trying to
figure out all you weren't saying, all you were withholding, all
you were hiding, all the secrets you were keeping from me, all
your sins of omission.

Dot dot dot.

Tennessee Williams once said that when you are going through
a period of unhappiness, a broken heart, the loss of a loved one,
or some other "disorder" in your life, then writing is the only refuge. (I found this quote while searching for the Steinem one.) I
would like this to be true. I would like writing to be my refuge, my
anchor, my salvation. Once, it was all of those things.

But during the height (or the depth) of my misery, I couldn't
even read for more than twenty minutes at a stretch, let alone
write anything other than more e-mails to you. I couldn't focus.
I couldn't concentrate. The words flew around in circles on the
page. I would read the same sentence over four or five times
and still it wouldn't make sense. By the time I reached the end
of a page, I couldn't remember what I'd read at the beginning.
This must have been why my father had to give up reading as his
Alzheimer's progressed. The simplest story escaped me, and soon
I'd find myself staring off into space or pacing around the house
in a fever of anxiety and fear.

Apparently, I have no refuge.

Words fail me.
Or I fail them.

✍

Write very slowly.
Write very quickly.
Write very large.
Write very small.
Write with red ink (or purple or green).
Write with your other hand.
Write on colored paper.
Write upside down.
Write in the dark.
Write in invisible ink.

✍

I began to worry that all the horoscopes I was sending you might be becoming an annoyance. I asked if you wanted me to cease and desist.

You said, No, no, please don't stop . . . I love receiving them! I figure I need all the help I can get in understanding my own life!

YOURS: All things must change. Nothing in life is permanent. Once you come to terms with this fact, you won't be quite so concerned about maintaining the status quo, either in your personal life or at work. It's okay to have doubts. It's okay to wonder if what you've done with your life has been worth it. But don't let those doubts paralyze you.

YOURS: Life is too short to waste time worrying about what other people might think of your behavior. If you have a yearning to do something that is going to set tongues wagging, do it and to hell with the consequences. You don't want to look back ten years from now and regret that you were not more adventurous.

MINE: Your attitude is a bit negative at the moment. Why is that? Whatever the reason, you must trust that everything will work out for the best in the end, even though right now you cannot see how that is going to happen.

MINE: It does not matter how many obstacles are placed in your path, or how tall they might be. You have what it takes to climb over them all. Fate will never ask you to do more than you are capable of, so don't worry if the mountain in front of you looks huge. You will find a way to move it.

✍

Early on, I used to send you bits and pieces of articles I'd read in the newspaper. This happened most often on a Monday morning, as I found the weekend papers full of things I knew you'd be interested in or amused by. I knew you weren't as much of a newspaper reader as I am: you said you never had the time.

I sent you stories about Tuscany and other places we'd talked of visiting together someday: New York City, Mexico, Paris, Alaska, the Caribbean on a cruise ship.

I sent you articles from the Careers section with titles like "Rules to win the networking game," "Improving your presentation skills,"

"What every employer really wants," and "Leverage your natural talents for maximum success."

I sent you a piece called "House sparrow in Aisle 2" about the growing problem of birds taking up residence in big-box stores in North American cities. The article said that a hawk had moved into a Home Depot store in Ohio and was feeding off the pigeons that also lived there. And apparently there was a flock of barn swallows at a Home Depot in Minneapolis that had learned how to operate the automatic doors by flying in front of the motion sensors!

I sent you the story of a Scottish woman with a lilting brogue who went to bed one night with a headache and woke up the next morning speaking with a South African accent. And there was the blind man in Romania who was arrested twice in one month for stealing a car. Not to mention the British pole-dancer who had to quit her job because she turned out to be allergic to the nickel in the pole. Or the Finnish man, already a father of six, who was so worried about impregnating his wife yet again that he put on a condom with super glue.

I sent you the full text of an article about the mental and physical health benefits of laughter. It was called "A laugh a day keeps the doctor away," and it discussed a new study which demonstrated that laughing provides much the same vascular benefits as aerobic exercise. The authors recommended thirty minutes of exercise three times a week plus fifteen minutes of laughter per day to achieve the maximum health benefits of both.

I sent you the story of a couple who'd been reunited after sixty years. They'd been high school sweethearts but were separated when he went off to fight in World War II. They lost touch. After the war, they both married other people, both of these spouses now deceased. They had seven children between them (four for her, three for him) and thirty-three grandchildren. Two weeks after they were reunited, they got married. She was seventy-seven and he was two months shy of his eightieth birthday. Now they both said it was as if they'd never been apart.

You said, That's a very nice story.

✒

I said, Yesterday was a long day in which many things that should have been simple were complicated, many other things that should have been pleasant were frustrating and annoying, and still more things that should have taken ten minutes took two hours! It was one of those days. And apparently I wasn't the only one. When I went downtown to the post office, I saw a young couple having a screaming argument on the corner. She was so mad she threw her bicycle at him!

I said, I didn't write to you yesterday because I wanted to spare you all my cranky whining. By the end of the day, I was headachy and exhausted and depressed by my own bad mood.

But, I said, having yesterday allowed myself to sink down into the slough of despond where I felt very vulnerable and forlorn (O ye of little faith, why are you still so afraid?), today I'm going to perform a miracle instead! Today I'm going to sprout wings and fly up to that sublime utopia where a new furnace does not cost six thousand dollars, where there is never a lineup at the bank or the post office, where all drivers are competent and courteous at all times, where there is always a parking space exactly where you need one, where soul mates who were meant to be together actually *are* together. I am, through sheer force of will, going to be a positive and happy person all day long!

You said (as you'd said many times before), You are such a good writer! Words just seem to flow so easily for you. You are so lucky. I envy you that.

I did not say, Luck has nothing to do with it. I spend hours and hours working on these damn e-mails to you.

I said, Thank you.

✍

Early on, I used to send you poetry. I would often spend the whole evening searching for the perfect poem to send you first thing in the morning. Sometimes I sent poetry when I didn't have anything interesting to write about. But sometimes, I confess, I sent you poems with a message, trusting that the poets could say it better and more subtly than I ever could.

Twice I sent you these lines from "Wild Geese" by Mary Oliver:

You do not have to be good.
You do not have to walk on your knees
for a hundred miles through the desert, repenting.
You only have to let the soft animal of your body
  love what it loves.
Tell me about despair, yours, and I will tell you mine.

The first time I sent you this was in the fall on a day when I'd had lunch in my backyard with Kate and Michelle, and we saw

six flocks of geese heading south while we ate black bean quesa-
dillas and drank mango juice and marveled at the fact that another
summer was already over. The sight of the geese filled me with the
same lush mix of emotions that it always does. Kate recited this
poem from memory, and then I sent it to you late that evening, so
it would be there waiting when you got to work the next morning.

You said, Thank you. I do so love all that you send me. You have
reawakened my interest in all that is poetic . . . and romantic.

You said, For all the thousands of words I see every day, it will
be yours and the verses you dispatch to me that I will remember
for all time.

I sent you these same lines again one afternoon in the spring
when I was alone in my backyard, cleaning up the mess that winter
had left behind. The geese were heading back north. There were
hundreds of them in two gigantic straggling flocks, one behind
the other, and the sound of their calls as they flew over made my
heart ache with loneliness.

I said, Remember when I sent you this poem in the fall? Now
the geese are back again. Time goes by and life goes on . . .

You did not reply.

✍

You said there was going to be a political protest in your city,
when the president of a country known for its human rights viola-
tions came to visit. You said you were planning to participate. I'd
seen news of this planned demonstration on television. They said
they were afraid there would be violence. A thousand extra police
officers were being called in.

As it turned out, you weren't able to attend after all, because of work demands that day.

In response to this information I said, I'm relieved that you couldn't go. I would have been so worried! I've never been involved in such a protest myself, but I think the potential for things getting out of hand was very great in this instance. Big crowds, strong emotions: a volatile combination.

You said, I'm very disappointed that I could not go to the protest. It may be true that the pen is mightier than the sword, but writers need something to write about and sometimes action needs to be taken, statements need to be made physically. I have been active in such matters of civil disobedience since I was sixteen years old and that will not change. In fact, as time goes on, I will probably become more involved than ever. You need never be concerned about me . . . I always keep my feet on the ground. I would take safety precautions, certainly . . . . . but I fear no situation.

I did not say, You should.

I said, Your implication that writers sit around on their asses all day doing nothing, while people who *really* care get out there and do something, is insulting to me. I feel as if you were putting me in my place in no uncertain terms. If the protest was that important to you, why didn't you just take time off work and go . . . instead of lashing out at me?

You said, I certainly did not mean to insult you or to infer that you are not involved in important issues. It seems that one of the problems with communicating by e-mail is that sometimes the tone comes out all wrong. In this case, it's this tone thing that has caused you to think I was lashing out at you.

I said, Yes, it's true that e-mail communication does have its limitations.

I did not say, If you were a better writer, you'd have a handle on this "tone thing" by now.

I said, Sometimes I'm confused. My "hotel lover" is so very different from my "e-mail lover." I like the hotel lover a whole lot more . . . he lavishes all his love and attention on me, and he makes me feel so special and loved. But the e-mail lover all too often feels like a complete stranger to me, not like a lover at all. He frustrates me because he doesn't answer my questions and his voice is very different and not so loving. I must figure out how to keep these two lovers together as one person in my head!

You said, It does trouble me that I cannot always express myself properly and freely to you. But the point being is that I am in an open-concept office here, stuck in a warren of gray cubicles with people wandering in and out. I am always conscious of this being a work e-mail that should not be used for personal correspondence. Plus there is some sense that e-mails are not entirely private, but I am not certain about that.

You said, All the more reason to look forward to your next visit . . . when we can talk freely, without interruptions or constraints.

You said, I know that for you and I, expressing what we truly think and feel is so very important . . . . . essential.

I said, I'm so afraid of losing you again.

You said, You are never going to lose me. I'm right here. I'm not going anywhere. I will always be here for you.

✍

I said I would always love you, no matter what happened. I said I would never turn my back on you, or wish I didn't love you so much.

I said, Knowing that you love me has changed how I am in the world.

I said, You enhance and enrich my life every single day, even on the most difficult days.

I said, The connection between us is eternal and indestructible.

I said, Although we've often said that nothing ever stays the same, there is one thing that will never change and that is my love for you.

✍

Later: I said, It seems that many of the things we've said to each other have turned out to be not entirely true. I guess we were right when we said nothing ever stays the same.

✍

Again, we were writing back and forth about my next impending visit, another business trip.

I said, Isn't it amazing how suddenly all roads lead to your city? Sometimes it seems that the universe is working in our favor!

You said, Yes, it's so wonderful. Hopefully I won't have to go to a meeting that night.

I said, If they do attempt to foist something on you for that evening, I trust you will politely but firmly explain that you have other pressing business that needs tending to (that means me!).

I said, Should I wear my fancy-dancy high-heeled black boots, which are quite fetching, or should I wear my sensible low-heeled boots, which are quite warm but not nearly so cute???

You said, There is still snow on the ground here.

I said, I think I'll wear the fancy boots anyway.

Afterwards you said, I'm really glad you wore those sexy boots.

I said, I'm really glad you didn't go to that meeting tonight.

✍

I am thinking about all the times you said you would call me and you didn't.

When I complained, you said you had to finish the quarterly budget report by the end of the day. You said, I have been chained to my desk here! I closed off my e-mails and my phone, shut my door, put my head down, and cranked out this material!

Or you said you'd been called away to a meeting that lasted all day and then you had another meeting in the evening. Or you said you'd been ensconced in a dimly lit room with your colleagues for an information session that lasted all day. Or you said you'd been hunkered down in a planning seminar that lasted all day. Or you said you had to finish a funding proposal by the deadline, which was the end of the day. Or you said there'd been a parade of people and phone calls there all day, and you hadn't had the luxury of an opportunity to be in touch with me. Or you said you'd been sequestered for four days charting out the next few weeks of work.

Or you said you'd been called in for your annual job review and it had taken all afternoon.

You said, I've been out working in the field, trying to stay away from my desk as much as possible!

You said, An essential part of the week has been impacted because of external demands.

You said, I am now tasked with more stuff, have been told to really focus and push everything else off to the side.

You said, I have been really inundated here with people dumping more work on me!

You said, I am under the gun here, trying to catch up on some important matters that need my immediate attention!

You said your building had lost its water supply. You said there had been freezing rain there all day. You said you had food poisoning. You said you had been unexpectedly required to attend an out-of-town symposium for three days. You said your dog died. You said you had the flu. You said you had been facilitating a conference for a day and a half. You said you had to have dental surgery and it took all week to recuperate. You said you'd thought about calling, but by then it was so late and you didn't want to wake me. You said your uncle died. You said you had the flu. You said you'd been doing home renovations all weekend (drywalling, sanding, priming, painting, painting, and more painting!). You said you fell asleep.

You said, I have been very ill. I was smitten by the horrible flu that is going around here, a most virulent strain of the virus! I felt like I just wanted to crawl under a rock.

You said, This is the first time all month that I've felt somewhat normal . . . that was the worst flu I've ever had! For gosh sakes, make sure you take your vitamins . . . this one hurts!

I did not say, I have not had a serious case of the flu for ten years.

I did not say, You get the flu more often than anybody else I've ever known in my life.

I said, Get a flu shot.

You said your cat died. You said your aunt died. You said a friend you'd known since high school died. You said a former colleague had died last week.

For months it seemed that I was always sending you letters of sympathy and condolence and support.

I said, I wish I could be there to comfort you.

I said, Please remember that my heart is always with you.

I said, You've had so much loss to deal with in the past few months. I wish I could do more to help you.

When I told Michelle about all of this, she said, The theme of this whole relationship is death.

I said, Good God!

When I asked Kate what all this death could possibly mean, she said, impatiently, It doesn't *mean* anything . . . it just *is*.

When I asked you if you had developed some kind of aversion to calling me, you said, Noooooo . . . . . no aversion . . . I've just been so busy.

You said, I fully intended to call you last week, but I was all over the city attending meetings and doing site visits. These days there just aren't very many pay phones around anymore . . . and they're all outside! They're either stuck to the side of a Tim Hortons or in some flimsy Plexiglas booth where the doors swing open and the wind whistles right through!

This was in January.

When I told Kate this, she snorted and said, Doesn't he have a *coat?*

You said you were going to get a cellphone so you could call me from anywhere anytime.

I said, Yes, good idea.

I did not say, Yes, it's about time you joined the twenty-first century.

I said, I don't think I'm asking for a lot. And yet even the little I'm asking for seems to be too much.

You said you had so many responsibilities and obligations just now. You said everyone was counting on you. You said you couldn't let them down.

You said, Hopefully I will return back to somewhat of a normal existence here next week. I promise to try and communicate better then . . . when I will hopefully have more time.

I said, Don't worry about me. I'm fine.

☛

You said you had never been under so much pressure in your entire life.

I said I thought a lot about all the pressure you were under. I said I wanted to make your life easier, not harder. I said I wanted to be the least of your worries. I said I never wanted to be a burden to you.

You said, I never want to be a burden to you either.

I said, You're not.

I said, Like Dr. Phil always says, I want to be your "soft place to fall."

You said, Who is Dr. Phil?

One day early on, after blathering on at length about some program I'd watched on TV the night before, I asked you what your favorite TV show was, and you told me that you didn't watch television, that you didn't even *own* a television set anymore. Being an incorrigible and unabashed devotee of the small screen myself, I found this so completely inconceivable that I didn't actually believe you.

And if, when you said it, there was in your voice that tone of superiority some people who don't watch television adopt toward those of us who do, I chose to overlook it.

✍

I am thinking about all the times you said you would send me an e-mail and you didn't.

I am thinking about how your silences began to stretch out longer and longer: four days, a week, ten days, two weeks, three. Clearly, the daily e-mails we used to have had fallen by the wayside, at least on your end. At first I wrote to you every day anyway, whether I heard back from you or not. And every time I finally did hear from you again after one of these silences, I wrote back immediately. It took me a long time to realize that every time I did this, every time I clicked on that Send button, I had put myself right back into the same position again: waiting.

Still waiting.

Always waiting.

Waiting and waiting and then waiting some more.

No matter what else I was doing, I was really just waiting to hear from you.

Here I was, alternating between fits of fury and fear, checking the obituaries to see if you were dead, calling your office just to make sure your voice was still there, because surely if you were dead, they would have changed your message . . . right?

Here I was thinking, after three and a half long silent weeks, You'd bloody well better be dead.

Here I was, writing still more e-mails, funny at first, then increasingly furious and/or frantic:

Twinkle twinkle little star, how I wonder where you are?

Are you there? Blink once for yes, twice for no!

Are you okay?

Is something wrong?

I don't mean to nag but . . . did you get my last letter?

I don't mean to nag but . . . why haven't you replied?

I don't mean to nag but . . . where the hell are you?

I can't take this anymore.

I cannot bear it when you leave me dangling here like this.

Why are you doing this to me?

Your silence is deafening.

Here I was, blowing a gasket: What the hell is going on there? I cannot help but imagine the worst. Either that or you've decided to discontinue this correspondence without telling me. Can that be true? Maybe. I don't know. I know nothing. You haven't replied to my many e-mails and you haven't responded to my phone messages either. I am pretty much at the end of my rope with trying to figure this out.

Here I was, begging: Please please just write me a quick note, however brief, to let me know you are okay.

Here I was, humiliated and appalled at myself for having begged: I've had enough. This will be my final attempt to contact you.

And then finally you would resurface, usually with the breezy subject line *Back!*

You said, No, I have not entirely disappeared from the face of this planet!

You said, I seem to have fallen off the ledge . . .

You said, I seem to have dropped off the map . . .

You said, I feel out of the loop with everything . . .

You said, I feel like I've gone into another zone . . .

You said, I feel like a bit of a lost boy here . . . again!

You said your e-mail had a glitch. You said your computer was down. You said your computer crashed every time you tried to access your e-mail. You said the IT people had adjusted your network connection and then it didn't work at all and it took them a week to come back and fix it. You said you'd written to me last week, but you made a mistake typing in my address and your letter was returned.

You said you'd sent me an e-mail last Friday and another one on the weekend, but apparently I hadn't received them. You said, I wonder where they went?

You said you'd written to me yesterday, but when you turned

your computer back on this morning, it said the message had been "timed out." You said, What does that mean?

You said, I sent you letters on Thursday and Friday. I'm wondering what the heck happened as they show up as being sent, and yet it seems you didn't receive them. So here goes again!

You said, I wrote to you early this morning, pushed Send, but then my computer did a funny freeze thing . . . and my letter vanished. Hopefully this one makes it through!

I said, Get a new computer.

You said it wasn't all about me.

I did not say, I realize that . . . but couldn't it be all about me once in a while?

You said I wasn't the only one you'd been letting down as far as regular contact went. You said your work colleagues had also been wondering where you were.

I did not say, Bully for them.

When I asked if you were feeling withdrawn these days, you said, Noooooo . . . . . not withdrawn . . . don't let those alarm bells of yours go off again . . . I've just been so busy.

You said, It was another week that was more than haphazard.

You said you thought that having a gap in our communication might actually help me get on with my writing.

You said, I never intended to be out of touch for so long . . . but time just went whooshing by . . . . . and things happened . . .

I said, What things?

You said, I do sincerely apologize for my scattered behavior . . . I am running on adrenaline these days.

You said, I feel like that cat on a hot tin roof . . . jumping from one thing to another all the time. Hopefully I can get back to some regularity here soon.

I did not say, You know they have effective laxatives for that these days.

You said, Getting back on track in communicating with you is so very important for my heart and soul. I promise I will write to you this weekend . . . if I have the space and time . . .

Many days passed.

I said, Apparently you have neither the space nor the time.

I said, I am so frustrated that I feel like I might as well be living in Siberia instead of just a couple of hours down the road.

I did not say, I'm sure that even in Siberia they have reliable e-mail by now. In the past month, thanks to the wonders of modern technology, I have received e-mails from Moscow, Kyoto, Oslo, a campground in the northern Wisconsin woods, a beach in Bermuda, and a ship traversing Davis Strait from the west coast of Greenland to the east coast of Baffin Island.

You said you knew your inability to communicate at times was frustrating and annoying for me, but that you were always thinking of me. You said that even when you weren't able to be in touch, still you loved me just as much.

You said, I have missed our ongoing contact so very much. But please know that my thoughts have certainly been wending their way to you.

You said you were always sending me your love by telepathy. I said, That's nice, but, at this end, my telepathy isn't working.

You said you could understand why I was angry. You said you were sorry for causing me concern and disruption and stress. You said you loved me so much and never wanted to cause me any worry or anxiety. You said you were so distressed with yourself for having done so . . . again.

You said, I have never meant to hurt you . . . again.

I said, I have started taking antidepressants . . . again.

You said nothing about this in your reply a week later. You wrote instead about the twenty-four different projects you were now working on, about a horrific car accident you'd seen on the way to work yesterday but fortunately nobody was seriously injured although this was hard to believe considering the look of the mangled wreckage, about a young man with dreadlocks you'd met in the park during your lunch-hour walk and he was carrying a binder filled with all the lyrics of Bob Marley written out by hand and he had memorized every single one of them!

You said, You will be pleased to know that this week I reorganized all my files . . . they were such an embarrassment! You said you'd followed the system I'd suggested months ago. You said how good it felt to have this finally done. You said, You always were a genius at organization! I am now looking at a neat row of gleaming banker's boxes . . . I can only say . . . what a relief!

You pledged that you would be better at communication from now on.

You promised.

You said you truly wanted to renew meaningful and consistent contact with me.

You said you were so sorry for hurting me, but you needed a bit more understanding.

I did not say, How the hell do you expect me to understand?

Most of what you say to me is so oblique and ambiguous and indirect that afterwards I don't know what you've really said anyway.

I did not say, I have been turning myself inside out and upside down trying to understand . . . enough already.

I said, All is forgiven.

Again.

☞

I am thinking about that old saying, the curse of the lovelorn: "Hope springs eternal."

I've looked it up and discovered that this is originally from Alexander Pope's "An Essay on Man": *Hope springs eternal in the human breast: Man never is, but always to be blest.*

This was written in 1733, almost three centuries ago. And yet, old as it may be, still it is predated by another saying, this one from the Bible, Proverbs 13:12: *Hope deferred maketh the heart sick.*

My friend Lorraine has a saying on this topic too: "I've given up all hope and I feel a lot better now." This is what I am currently striving for. So far it isn't working.

Interestingly enough, it was also Alexander Pope who wrote, *Fools rush in where angels fear to tread.*

☞

After all your problems with computers and telephones, I wanted to make it as easy as possible for you to be in touch with me. So I bought a book of postcards, thirty historical views of your city rendered in sepia tones. I put a stamp on each postcard and carefully printed my own name and address in the space below.

I thought this was very clever. I gave the postcard book to you as a gift.

We were in the lobby of the luxury hotel at the time. Marble floors, mahogany walls, antique end tables, richly upholstered sofas and chairs, a crystal chandelier the size of a small car sparkling down upon well-dressed men and women going about their business with aplomb.

We were admiring a series of photographic portraits of famous people that were hung around the lobby. You stared thoughtfully for a long time at a photo of Georgia O'Keeffe. I began to chatter on about a lengthy biography of her I'd once read and how much I'd always loved her paintings.

You said, It's a wonder nobody tries to steal these.

I said, They're bolted to the wall.

We sat down on one of the elegant sofas. I pulled the postcard book from my bag and handed it to you.

I said, When you're not able to send me an e-mail or call me, now you can send me a postcard instead!

You were silent. You looked through the cards carefully, examining each photograph slowly and in detail, as if that were the point of it: the pictures.

Finally, you put them in your briefcase and said, What exactly are you going to do with these postcards when I send them?

As if you thought I was going to run all over town with them or have them printed in the newspaper or posted on the Internet or something.

You said, Are you going to put them on the fridge?

I said, No.

I received three postcards from you in the following month and then no more. Kate and I joked that, just as your city was short on pay phones, apparently there were no mailboxes there either.

I teased you about this. I said, You know those big red square metal things frequently located on street corners . . . find one!

You said you loved the pictures on the postcards so much that you wanted to keep them for yourself.

I said, For me, any day that I hear from you is automatically a better day than one in which I don't.

The next day, you sent me a long cheery e-mail about all your future plans, hopes and dreams, prospects and possibilities.

You said, I have such a strong inner drive to accomplish so much.

I could not help but notice that apparently you thought you were going to live forever.

I could not help but notice that I did not appear in any of this.

(I also could not help but notice that, in this case, *not* hearing from you would have made for a better day after all.)

I said, When I allow myself to look into the future, you are always there front and center.

You said, It is important to focus on the here-and-now, to take it one day at a time, so let's stay on that track . . .

You said, It is a step-by-step process.

Sometimes I tried not to write to you so often. At one point, I checked back through the growing stack of our correspondence and discovered that, since we'd spent that first night together at the luxury hotel, the longest I'd gone without writing to you was six days. I figured that if I didn't write so often, this would give you time to miss me.

I wanted you to have some sense of what it felt like to be the one waiting. I thought it would do you good to suffer a bit, as I'd been suffering. I thought you would appreciate me more if I wasn't always right there chirping away at you, regular as rain. I thought you might actually pay more attention to me if you thought you might lose me.

At the time, I thought that if I wasn't always so reliable and predictable, you would actually notice.

Now I think: If you did notice, you were probably relieved.

✎

I said, It is not good for me to be feeling that I am always last on your list of things to do. And that I am always the one thing that can be dispensed with.

You did not reply.

I said, It is not good for me to be feeling that I am no longer even *on* your list of things to do.

You said, My days seem to shift like blowing dune sand on a windswept Atlantic shore . . .

✎

I said, Although you are the most important thing in my life right now, I often feel that I am just a speck in yours.

You said, You are not a speck.

✍

I said, It seems the only time I can get your attention is when I'm freaking out.
You did not reply.

✍

I said, It seems that even when I'm freaking out, still I cannot get your attention anymore.
You did not reply.

✍

I said, I need some reassurance from you, and I need it *now*. You said a while back that we were in this together. But now I feel like I'm in this all by myself. This seems like cruel and unusual punishment to me. Right now I just want to hear you talk. About anything. It doesn't matter what. We don't have to talk about anything emotional or upsetting. I just need to hear your voice.

You said, I can appreciate everything you say. Yes, we are overdue for a phone call. I long to hear your voice too. I will hopefully get back to you later.

By this point, I had already learned that when you said "hopefully," chances were it would never happen.

By this point, I had finally realized that you were never going to learn how to use the word *hopefully* correctly.

By this point, I was beginning to see that you were not so unpredictable after all.

I am thinking about how you were always saying:

This has been a blur of a week.

Another week . . . another blur of activities.

This has been a blur of a month.

These past few months have been a blur.

You said, Migosh, how time has zipped by! Working extra hours at both ends of the day, my life has become a blur . . . full, but chaotic!

I am thinking about how you once said that we existed in such different worlds. This had bothered me.

At the time, I said, No, I don't think so. I think we just happen to live in different parts of the *same* world.

Now I say: Yes, we do live in different worlds. Yours is much blurrier than mine. Perhaps you need glasses.

Sometimes the newspaper horoscopes, like the crossword puzzle clues, seemed to be uncannily applicable to our situation.

YOURS: As the sun moves into one of the more sensitive areas of your chart today, you must expect some people in your life to be more touchy than usual. You will be touchy too, so try not to overreact to what you perceive to be other people's obstinacy and ill-humor.

YOURS: You will amaze friends and even family members who

thought they knew everything about you. Whatever you get up to this week, it will change the way other people look at you, and maybe even the way you look at yourself.

MINE: You may want to give someone who has let you down a second chance, but is that really such a good idea? It is important that you are able to trust people, and the sad fact is that this is not the first time this person has failed to deliver. If you do give them another chance, make sure they know that this time it really is all or nothing.

YOURS: Before this day is over, you will realize that the confusion you have been feeling of late is because you have been looking at your existence from the wrong angle. Something you see or hear over the next twenty-four hours will answer many of your questions and set you off in a new direction that lasts a lifetime.

☞

I am thinking about how sometimes I still catch myself thinking of things I want to tell you, but we are no longer in touch and so I don't. Things like:

Last week I bought two new fridge magnets with illustrations of elegant mink-collared women from the forties with flawless skin, deep red lipstick, and eyebrows plucked into shrewd ironic arches. One magnet says, *She knew how to please a man but most days she chose not to.* The other says, *Rainy days and morons always get me down . . .* (It was the ellipsis in this one, as much as the sentiment, that made me laugh out loud in the store.)

One day I was stopped at a red light downtown in a rainstorm. A huge tour bus came lumbering through the intersection and turned left in front of me. It was completely covered with one of those wraparound advertising signs. The picture on the bus featured a majestic castle, so vivid and clear, even in the rain, that it was virtually three-dimensional. It was not until the light had turned green and I was on my way again that I realized the building on the bus was the luxury hotel in your city in which we'd stayed together. When I got home after doing my errands, I was hardly even surprised to find an e-mail from the hotel called *Customer Satisfaction Survey.*

I heard "Dancing in the Moonlight" three times in one week. The first two times I heard it on the oldies radio station I always listen to in the car. The first time, I cried, but only lightly, only briefly, only a little bit, not enough to have to pull over. The second time, I turned off the radio and sailed on to my destination with only a small lump in my throat and a barely noticeable knot in my stomach.

The third time I heard the song I was in a downtown restaurant having lunch with my friend Lorraine. After much unnecessary studying of our menus, we ordered the same thing we always had: steak sandwiches for both of us (hers rare, mine medium), french fries, corn salsa, garlic mayonnaise for dipping, and unlimited cups of decaf. The song came on while we were waiting for our food.

At the sound of the opening bars, I stopped talking in midsentence and pointed at the ceiling from where the music was emanating. We both listened intently for a moment, our heads tilted upwards. Then we pursed our lips, rolled our eyes, and picked up our conversation where we'd left off.

By the time our steak sandwiches arrived, we had forgotten all about you.

✍

I am thinking about the last time I saw you. I was once again in your city staying at the luxury hotel.

An hour or so before it was time for me to leave and come home, we decided to have a drink in the lobby piano bar. I had coffee, you had a glass of red wine which, I couldn't help but note, cost nearly as much as a whole bottle would in the liquor store. We held hands across the table, while making inconsequential easy talk as comfortably as if we did this every day.

At one point, I went to the washroom and enjoyed the sensation of you watching me as I walked across the room. With my fancy-dancy high-heeled black leather boots, I was wearing a new outfit (an exceptionally sleek-fitting knee-length black skirt and a shimmering turquoise silk shirt that clung in all the right places) that I'd bought especially for this visit, not for the business I had to do, but for you. Up in the room, you had duly admired and then gently removed it, one piece at a time, beginning with the boots.

Soon it was time for me to go. You paid for our drinks and I retrieved my suitcase from the concierge desk. You said you wished you could drive me to the train station, but you really had to get back to work. So you put me and my suitcase in a taxi and told the driver to take good care of me. He smirked at me in the rearview mirror as we pulled away and you stood there waving sadly.

I didn't cry in the taxi, as I didn't want to give the driver the satisfaction. But I did cry at the train station. Nobody much seemed to notice. Those few people who did notice didn't seem to mind. Several women smiled at me with instinctive sympathy and understanding. I had an epiphany about the fact that there are a goodly number of public places in which crying is acceptable, train stations definitely being one of them, also bus depots, airports, churches, hospitals, cemeteries, movie theaters, and possibly bars very late at night after half a dozen drinks and a few too many sad songs (although not in grocery stores, as I had already ascertained). I wrote all this down in the little notebook I carry in my purse (just like writers are supposed to).

Then I called you at work from my cellphone to tell you my epiphany. I was still crying. You answered, but you were busy and couldn't talk.

I boarded the train at the appropriate time. Somewhere in the shuffle of finding my seat, stowing my suitcase, and giving my ticket to the conductor, I stopped crying. When we hadn't started moving forty-five minutes past the scheduled departure time and were already getting restless, they announced that the train was broken.

We sat there in the station for another two hours, which was about as long as my trip home should have taken. We sat there eating tiny bags of peanuts and potato chips, watching the sun go down in the west. I rested my head against the window while your city was swallowed into the darkness and then began to sparkle in the night.

There was a lot of grumbling and sighing, many disgruntled passengers on their cellphones calling home to say they would be late. I had no one at home to call. I thought about calling Kate or Michelle, but then I decided to call you again instead. This time there was no answer.

Finally they hooked our train up to another train (this took some time, as you can imagine) and towed it all the way back to my city and beyond.

Of course I told you all this in an e-mail the next morning.

You said, Train trips are poignant and reflective enough . . . but to have that long delay on top of it all! I certainly empathize and feel for you. I wish very much I could of been at the station, but that too can be a hard thing . . . so many old movies had partings at train stations. . . . Still, it would have been really nice to have had that extra time together.

I didn't know then that this would be the last time we saw each other.

Did you?

I thought we would just go on and on.

Did you?

✍

There were so many questions I asked that you never answered. But there are still some very important questions that, for some reason, I never had the nerve to ask. Questions to which I would still like to know the answers, although I'm sure I never will now.

I would still like to know when you decided we were done.

I would still like to know why you never bothered to mention this to me. I would still like to know why you just let me go on and on.

133

✍

I am thinking about the last time I saw you.
You said I was perfect.
I said you were perfect too.
We were both naked. We were both wrong.

✍

Write a story that begins with the question, "Why didn't you call me?"
Write a story that begins with the question, "Why didn't you write to me?"
Write a story that begins with the question, "Why didn't you tell me you didn't want me anymore?"

✍

Write a story in the form of a love letter.
I am.

✍

I am thinking about how many times I told you I'm a person who needs to know the truth no matter what it is.
You said you respected and admired this so very much.

✍

Write about silence.
Write about a forbidden activity.
Write about electricity.

Write about regret.
Write about dubious intentions.
Write about casting a spell.
Write about cowardice.
Write about lies.
Write about mistaken identity.
Write about a promise made.
Write about a promise broken.
Write about crying.
Write one whole page about snot.

✍

I said, In my romantic dream of our story, I am indeed an angel, able to handle this situation forever with grace and ease and strength, thinking only of you and never of myself. In my romantic dream, I am serene and selfless, always giving, never needing anything more than the sheer joy of loving you, even when I don't hear from you for weeks, even when I don't see you for months on end. But in reality, I'm disappointed to discover that I am none of these things. Not serene. Not selfless. Not able to keep giving without wanting something in return. Still not able to conquer this communication issue. Still not able to stop wanting to hear your voice and see your face. In reality, I'm disappointed to discover that I am not an angel . . . I am just human.

I said, My romantic dream is so rich and beautiful and would make a very good movie. But reality is so different: so paltry and hopeless and impossible. As you well know, love in the real world is never what you expect it to be.

You said, I want to stop hurting you.

❭

I said, Five or ten years from now, when we look back on this time in our lives, I wonder what we will say. How will we describe it? I guess time will tell . . . just as it always does.

You did not reply.

❭

When it became increasingly apparent that I wasn't managing the stress and anxiety of our situation especially well, you said I should take up running. You said this would help me get back to writing regularly. You said I wasn't getting enough exercise. You said medical studies have shown that fitter people are in better mental health and that exercise is now becoming a recognized treatment for anxiety and depression. You said that if I wanted to hang around with you, I had to become a practitioner of physical fitness.

You said, You already have the body of a runner . . . you would be a natural!

I said, If I do already have the body of a runner, then I've managed to get it without running. Why start now?

You said if I wasn't keen on running, then walking would be the next best thing. You said I should go out and buy myself a proper pair of walking shoes. You said, If you take up walking, then you too can consider yourself an athlete!

I bristled at your tone. I said I'd never had any great burning desire to consider myself an athlete.

You apologized for being so avuncular, a characteristic of yours that you said others had also objected to in the past.

Eventually I capitulated. I said that, resistant though I might have been to this idea initially, still I would give it a try . . . in my regular boots. It was February after all.

You said I should send you a daily progress report.

Day One

WALKING REPORT

From here to downtown and back: 1 hour round trip with 2 short stops. Purchased shampoo and conditioner at The Body Shop (very good: all-natural ingredients, community trade honey from Zambia, olive oil from Italy, not tested on animals) and an iced cappuccino at Tim Hortons (not so good: probably healthier to drink the shampoo . . . does consumption of iced cappuccino cancel out benefits and virtues of walk?). While walking, did not smoke, drink Pepsi, or talk on cellphone. Saw several other people walking while doing some or all of these things. Also saw one man eating a pizza slice. Appeared to be pepperoni and mushrooms, possibly also onions. Thought it better not to look too closely for fear of being misunderstood.

CONCLUSIONS

- Am supposed to be writing light-hearted book about happiness while feeling heavy-hearted and unhappy. Perhaps should write light-hearted book about unhappiness, heavy-hearted book about happiness, or heavy-hearted book about unhappiness. Many options!
- Walking is much easier than writing.

Day Two

WALKING REPORT

Drove downtown but then walked around doing errands: approx. 45 minutes. Does walking (quickly) while doing errands have same beneficial effects as walking for its own sake? Perhaps not as soothing but still good exercise?

Had some bad moments in art supply store brought on by song on Muzak featuring line: *Some people wait a lifetime for a moment like this . . .* Recovered with help of Bruce Springsteen on car radio while driving home. In song called "Dancing in the Dark" (as opposed to "Dancing in the Moonlight"), the Boss going on about how tired he is of sitting around here trying to write this book! Laughed out loud.

CONCLUSIONS

- Why do all stores play music? People no longer capable of shopping without soundtrack? Music is ubiquitous hazard. Must buy earplugs.
- Despite musical ambush, did feel weight of world lifting off skinny shoulders. Not sure if due to walking or to finally getting errands done. Either way, very good. Skinny shoulders not up to the task.

Day Three

WALKING REPORT

From here to Victoria Park and back: 35 minutes round trip with no stops. Despite umbrella, walk curtailed due to rain. Fog nice though. At park, three hockey rinks and family skating loop all melted. Very sad. (Remember when winter was cold and there was no such thing as rain in February?) Found a quarter and a teeny-tiny black-and-white plastic cow. Signs from God? Should make phone call? Should drink more milk? Should move to Alberta and become cattle baroness?

Post-walk bubble bath with lavender oil (said to be soothing fragrance): 30 minutes. Was briefly soothed.

CONCLUSIONS

- Writing this report most fun had all day.
- Walking still easier than writing, despite inclement weather. Felt very virtuous while putting one foot in front of the other.
- Combination of new shampoo and wet weather made hair look very nice.
- Too many baths in February, even with lavender oil, make skin very dry. Must return to Body Shop and buy moisturizer.

Day Four

WALKING REPORT

Did not walk. Lazy. Stomach upset. Headache. Too cold out. (Winter is back.) Feet hurt. Many excuses. Had nap instead. Post-nap pacing around house while trying to write: 1 hour and 45 minutes. (Can pacing be counted as walking?)

CONCLUSIONS

- Feel guilty.
- But not guilty enough to get out there.

Day Five

WALKING REPORT

No walk again today. Still too cold out. Would rather stay inside and read a book in front of fireplace. (Do not actually have fireplace, but would sit and read in front of it if I did. Will curl up under snuggly afghan instead.) While reading, will drink Pepsi and smoke. Later, will put on pajamas and housecoat, eat large bag of barbecue potato chips, drink more Pepsi, and watch trashy reality TV show in which one wealthy handsome bachelor must choose a wife from a bevy of twenty-five buxom babes.

CONCLUSIONS

- Not destined to be athlete.
- Have now officially opted for early retirement from walking career. Will stick to laughing instead. (See article: "A laugh a day keeps the doctor away.")
- Hope you are not mad at me.

You said you could understand my resistance to physical exercise. You said you knew how hard it was to change.

You said, Forging your own lifestyle is your domain and anything I offer or suggest is not a command by any means.

You said I could choose to ignore or accept. You said you certainly would not be judgmental about this.

You said, There are things we like or are comfortable with about ourselves and do not really want to change.

I said, I'm glad you understand.

You said, If we try to change each other, it will only end in disaster.

I said, I don't want to change you . . . I love you just the way you are.

You were supposed to say you didn't want to change me either, but you didn't.

Not surprisingly, my horoscope for the following day said: *You are who you are for good reasons and trying to change that is an exercise in futility. Once you understand this, your life will be easier by far, not least because you stop trying to please people whose personalities and paths through life are so different from your own.*

✍

I said, For years I thought I had my life all figured out. And a carefully constructed life it was, a life that allowed me to feel safe and sane and happy enough. Now I feel all in a muddle. I'm no longer fitting into my own life as well as I used to.

I said, I've always loved my little house. I've lived here for twenty years and I've always loved the comforting sense of having it wrapped around me. I've always loved all my stuff too, probably more than I should. I've always loved this little square inch of the planet that I call mine. I said, But lately I find myself wanting to get rid of everything. This little house is *so full of stuff*, it's a wonder it doesn't explode! Sometimes I imagine that the walls are bulging under the strain. Or that it's going to fall over to the one side where all the floor-to-ceiling bookshelves are. I feel burdened by so much stuff. Right now I would just like to get rid of everything and live in a white room with only the barest of necessities . . . or maybe in a tent or a cave or on an island accessible only by floatplane. There I would give my life to literature and leave the rest behind . . .

By "the rest" I meant you.

I wanted you to be alarmed at the thought that I might be quite capable of doing something drastic and dramatic like decamping and disappearing altogether, never to be seen or heard from again.

But I also wanted you to know that I was willing to give up everything if I had to . . . "if I had to" meaning if you asked me to come and live with you there.

(It occurs to me now that you were not then, or ever, much likely to be trying that hard to read between the lines of my so carefully drafted e-mails. It occurs to me now that you were not peering at my so painstakingly chosen words the way I was perpetually peering at your infuriating dot dot dots.)

Again, my horoscope for the following day was right on the money: *There is a lot of clutter in your life at the moment. Your most urgent task right now is to get rid of anything and anyone that doesn't take you closer to your long-term goals. Do it today.*

You said, I can certainly agree that over the years we do tend to accumulate a lot of clutter.

✍

Somewhere in the middle of all this, you suddenly stopped signing your e-mails with love. You started signing them with just your name instead, sometimes only your first initial. I was very upset. So I stopped signing my e-mails with love too.

This went on for two weeks.

Finally I asked, Why have you stopped signing your e-mails with love?

You said, Have I? I didn't realize I'd done that. I guess I just forgot.

I said, Didn't you notice that I stopped signing mine with love too?

You said, Well, no . . . I didn't.

After that you started signing your e-mails with love again.

And so did I.

✍

Write about these words that have multiple meanings: bear, cleave, lie, tear, desert.

Write about these words that have multiple interpretations: love, trust, truth, never, forever.

✍

I said, Sometimes I get very annoyed and impatient with myself for not always being able to handle this with equanimity. I keep thinking that one of these days I'm going to have the one magic thought that will make all my extravagant and unruly emotions more manageable. Sometimes I get so tired of feeling all these *feelings* all the time.

You said, Feelings . . . . . ah yes . . . sometimes I wish I could just banish them from my brain, for more often than not, they cause me more complexity than I wish to deal with . . . but then

I do not want to become the reverse, which would be "unfeeling," for that would be a banishment to some form of purgatory. I find, as time moves on, my emotions are much closer to the surface . . . . I thought I would be tougher as I got older, but I am finding the opposite is true.

☞

I told you I had a very bad cold, something rare for me. My throat was sore all the way up into my ears and I was feverish. I said I was feeling so lousy that yesterday I took some Tylenol and vitamin C and stayed in bed all day.

I said, Usually, when I don't feel well, I force myself to get up and get dressed and go through the motions anyway . . . but yesterday I surrendered! And I think there's hope for me today: not only can I breathe out of my right nostril, but my head seems to be only half-filled with concrete, and I no longer feel like I've been hit in the middle of the forehead with a brick! Clearly, recovery is proceeding apace!

You said, I feel very literary today! I think I'm going to write a book! I'll send you more on this when I have prepared a summary proposal for what I have in mind.

I said, Good for you! I'm very curious about your book idea and look forward to hearing more about it when you have something ready to show me. If I can be of any assistance in any way, please don't hesitate to ask!

I did not say, Good for you! I have not felt "literary" for months.

Diane Schoemperlen

☛

I told you that my neighbor had died, the one who'd recently turned ninety, the one for whom the bagpiper played "Scotland the Brave" in the street.

I said, I heard the ambulance arrive in the middle of the night. I got up to see what was happening. I saw them bring her out of the house on the stretcher, her face covered with a sheet.

You said, It is an absolutely glorious day here . . . soft, clear, bright, and filled with the spring songs of returning birds. It is one of those special mornings that fill you with appreciation, wonderment, and joy.

☛

I said, Last night we had a terrible storm here, the tail end of the weather system that brought tornadoes to areas west of here yesterday afternoon. The power was out for several hours and the wind was terrifying. I was so frightened that I went down to the basement with my flashlight and sat shivering in an old lawn chair until the lights came back on. A very large poplar tree about a block away was brought down around midnight, broken off right at the base. The sound was so loud I thought it was one of my own big trees in the backyard. Fortunately it fell into the street and not onto the people's house. But not everyone was so lucky. When I was out this morning, I saw trees down all over the city, some as large as three or four feet in diameter that had been snapped off not more than a foot above the ground. Several cars were crushed and homes damaged.

145

You said, This has been a very convoluted week here. Work has been interesting, diverse, and totally all-consuming. I am trying to keep all my balls juggling in the air.

I did not say anything about your balls.

✍

A couple of years ago, on my birthday, Michelle gave me a doll called "Mr. Wonderful." He is about a foot tall with a large plastic head, sculpted wavy brown hair, big blue eyes, and a huge smiling mouth full of miraculously white plastic teeth. He's wearing a light blue shirt and khaki pants with a brown leather belt. His feet are extremely large, shod in brown lace-up boots. He's very muscular in the shoulders and tiny in the waist. When you press on his left hand, he says all those wonderful things that women since time immemorial have allegedly been longing to hear:

Actually, I'm not sure which way to go. I'll just turn in here and ask for directions.

Honey, why don't you just relax and let me make dinner tonight? The ball game isn't really that important. I'd rather spend time with you.

Why don't we go to the mall? Didn't you want to get some new shoes?

Here, you take the remote. As long as I'm with you, I don't care what we watch.

Did you have a hard day, honey? Why don't you sit down and let me rub your feet?

You know, I think it's really important that we talk about our relationship.

He does not say:

I've been so busy . . .

Hopefully I'll have time to call you next week . . .

I had the flu again . . .

I couldn't find a pay phone . . .

I couldn't find a mailbox . . .

My e-mail had a glitch . . .

My computer was down . . . again.

For a long time I thought you were Mr. Wonderful.

Apparently you are not.

✍

I said, There are no easy answers. At the moment, there seem to be no answers at all.

You said, Quit worrying so much and get back to work, my dear.

I said, I'm not worrying, I'm thinking.

You said, Well, stop it, whatever you're doing, and get back to work!

I said, What is the difference between worrying and thinking?

You said, Things are really heating up here today . . .

I figured I might as well answer my own question, since you obviously weren't going to take a stab at it. I said, The difference between thinking and worrying is that when I'm thinking, I'm mulling things over, rolling them around in my mind so I can see them from different perspectives (not an unpleasant experience and frequently productive), but when I'm worrying, I'm fretting and fussing and getting myself all in a knot (not so pleasant, not so

147

productive, causes high anxiety, which then feeds on itself like a chain-reaction collision and just gets worse and worse).

You said, Holy smokes . . . you are so good at all this psychology stuff! I'm going to have to get a couch in my office here!

You said, But for now . . . I have to park it for a bit and keep my job in primary focus today. All this emotional stuff is negatively impacting my work performance. I have a backlog of people here waiting for my action on a number of things.

I did not reply.

✍

I said, If doing the right thing always felt good, and doing the wrong thing always felt bad, life would be a much simpler undertaking.

You did not reply.

✍

Even after things were becoming difficult between us, sometimes I still tried to amuse you. On a wet and gloomy Monday morning in late October, I downloaded a photograph of a steaming bowl of chili and sent it along.

I said, I made a big pot of chili here yesterday and thought you might like to have some for lunch today. Do you like sour cream on yours? I do.

You did not reply.

I guess you had other plans for lunch.

I was always saying, I'm doing much better now.

I was always making resolutions that I thought would help me get my life back in order.

I was always saying, I'm going to put all this upset behind me and go forward now in a more positive way.

I was trying to convince myself as much as you. I guess I thought that if I said it often enough, eventually it would be true.

I said, I suppose one of the hardest things about this for me is that no matter how well I think I've got things sorted out, they never stay sorted for long. Before I know it, they start shifting around all over again. I do hope I can settle into this more smoothly now, without so many rocky bits. What I wouldn't give (you too, I'm sure) for a good stretch of time without so many rocky bits!

I said, The only time I feel truly good is when I'm with you. Then I feel that finally I'm the person I was meant to be, the person I've always wanted to be. Since we're able to see each other so seldom, this poses a real problem for me!

You did not reply.

I said, I'm trying so hard to get my ducks in a row.

To Kate I said, Every time I get my damn ducks in a row, they get blown right out of the water again. Bloody feathers flying everywhere!

You said, I must get my ducks in a row here too.

I did not say, Quack quack.

✍

You said, I'm not the only guy in the world, you know.

We were on the phone. For once you'd actually called me when you said you would. Of course I was delighted to hear from you and we chatted amiably for a while. But then the conversation took a turn and I found myself complaining about how much I missed you, how hard I found it to be away from you, how much I needed to see you.

And then you said it: I'm not the only guy in the world, you know.

Like a child, I cried, Take it back, take it back, take it back!

You said, Forget I ever said it.

In the background I could hear the general hubbub of a busy office and the sound of another phone ringing.

Then I could hear typing.

I said, Are you typing while we're talking?

You said, Yes, I'm trying desperately to get caught up on things here.

✍

Sometimes the newspaper horoscopes seemed to be custom-made for the two of us.

MINE: By all means let your feelings show today, but don't go overboard and give others the impression that you are a slave to your emotions. At this time of year, more than most, you can be rather excitable, with the result that you may come across as something of a drama queen.

YOURS: People will waste your time today if you let them—so don't let them. You have too much to think about and too much to do to pay attention to what others are up to, nor do you have the physical or emotional energy to take care of their needs as well as your own. You don't always have to be the nice guy.

✍

Write about the first (or last) person who broke your heart. If you had the opportunity to take revenge, would you?

Revenge is such a nasty word . . .

✍

You said you'd been working out every day, walking too, even running sometimes, keeping up with your own physical fitness regimen. You said, See . . . I practice what I preach!

I said, Why can't I just get on with my life the way you're getting on with yours? I envy you that.

You took exception to this.

You said, It may look like I'm getting on with my life, but really I'm just going through the motions.

You said, I have no choice, I *have* to get on with my life.

You said, If I don't, the consequences will be dire!

As if the consequences of me not getting on with my life could only be negligible in comparison.

✍

We agreed that we both felt all of this was a test. But we weren't sure what we were being tested on.

I said, Maybe we're being tested on different things.

You said, Maybe.

I said, But why does it seem that my strength always has to be tested? Why can't God just look down on me and think, Okay, she's strong enough now, yup, she's passed enough tests, so I'll just leave her alone for a while and let her live in peace and happiness?

I said, Much as I don't think I really needed another big test in my life, still I'm determined to pass this one!

I said, I often think that if I'd been able to hang in there thirty years ago, things would have turned out differently. So I'm determined to hang in there this time, no matter what it takes. Although I'm not sure what this test is really all about, I do have a clear idea of how it will feel once it's been passed. All things come to she who will but wait . . .

You said, All in all, one thing remains constant . . . . . life is always full, complex, and continuously enlightening.

✍

A month had passed since our last visit. I'd only had four or five e-mails from you in the interim and not a single phone call.

I said, At the risk of regretting it, today I need to pour my heart out to you. It's been a whole month now since I was there. Time goes by and life goes on. Now I think it was all a dream after all. When I was there with you, I felt so loved. Why can't I keep that feeling when I'm back home here by myself? It seems that you keep getting further and further away. I don't feel connected to you at all these days. I feel so unloved. I feel that my attention to you is no longer desired or required. I feel that I should just leave you alone now. You are so withdrawn. I think I should also withdraw in response . . . but I can't seem to do it. This makes me feel like I'm throwing myself at you.

I said, I think I'm just not the right kind of person to be able to handle this very well. Maybe I'm too insecure, too demanding, too needy, too sensitive, too obsessive . . . too much in love . . . too *something*, that's for sure!

I said, Sorry about this . . . sorry if I'm whining . . . I probably shouldn't send this but I'm going to . . . I have to be open and honest . . . this is my curse.

You said, I do understand completely all that you say, and it troubles me so damned much that I have caused you to feel hurt and disconnected. If I could, I would love to be able to communicate all the time, anytime, freely. The last time I felt true joy and warmth and overall well-being was a month ago . . . with you.

I said, Thank you. For your understanding. And for being you. Thank you for being so patient with me. I love you so much.

You said, Thank you. I look forward to everything we will bring to each other this week, next week, and into the future . . . for the rest of our lives.

I said, Please don't think that every single day has been horrible for me here . . . I've had some good days too! I even kept track for a while, making a note in code in my Day-Timer at the end of each day:

VG = very good

G = good

M = medium or mixed

B = bad

VB = very bad

U = unbearable

I said, A few weeks ago I watched a television documentary about veterinarians. They were discussing how to decide when it's time to have your ailing animal put to sleep. They said that if your beloved pet is having more bad days than good, then it's time. I certainly did get to a point where I was having more bad days than good! But I'm doing a lot better now.

You said, I do not believe in euthanasia.

☞

You said you hadn't written to me for a few days because you were feeling so low and you didn't want to burden me with your problems.

I said, You never need to keep your problems or your feelings from me, no matter what they are. Please don't hide from me. I love you as much (or more) when you're feeling vulnerable and sad as I do when you're feeling strong and happy. You do not need to be Superman. I love you when you're resilient and steadfast. I love you when you're frustrated and anxious. I love you when you're certain. I love you when you have doubts. I love you when you're all mixed up. I love you when you're perfect. I love you even more when you're not.

I said, You once said I was very good at coaxing your true feelings out of you . . . I guess I'll just have to keep on doing that!

You said, It is not my nature to share my feelings and problems with everyone.

I said, I am not everyone.

You did not reply.

✍

I am thinking about Christmas. I sent you a package in early December: my current favorite CD, *Alina* by Arvo Pärt, which my friends and I were listening to all the time just then; a book of poetry, *Why I Wake Early* by Mary Oliver, author of the "Wild Geese" poem; a paperweight from Vietnam, a fist-sized black rock so polished and lacquered that it gleamed, two orange and red goldfish painted on it in such fine shimmering strokes that they appeared to be swimming.

In the card (which featured a sad-eyed slobbery Saint Bernard in a Santa suit saying, *I wish I could see you . . . with more than just my heart!*) I said I didn't want you to feel obligated to send me a present just because I'd sent you one. (Of course, I didn't exactly mean that.)

In an e-mail two weeks later, you thanked me for the lovely and thoughtful gifts (which you said you hadn't had a chance to open until now). You said that yes, you were indeed going to send me something too, not just one thing, but several things that you were now in the process of assembling.

I said, I'm so tickled . . . I'll await their arrival eagerly! I must confess . . . I do love presents, both giving and receiving them!

This was a week or so before the holidays. You said you hoped the package would find its way to me in time. I pictured you driving to the highway at the outskirts of your city and flinging the present out your car window in my general direction, wishing it Godspeed, safe journey on its way to me through ice and snow and traffic.

It never made it, thus joining the ranks of all the other things you said you'd send me that never arrived.

Kate and Michelle and I joked about this.

We said, The road to hell. Good intentions. Paved with. Dot dot dot.

We said, In this case, the road to hell is paved with wayward Christmas presents, unmailed postcards, allegedly sent e-mails, and unmade phone calls.

Not to mention that cellphone you never bought (or never called me from if you did buy it) and all those loving thoughts you said you had been sending me by telepathy.

It is July. Where is my present?

✍

I am thinking about how many things there are that if a writer puts them in a story with the right words, the right tone, and the right timing, they are very funny. But in real life, those very same things were devastating.

In the story, these things can make even the writer herself laugh, especially at her own foolishness and gullibility. But in real life, those very same things occasioned excessive tears, obsessive soul-searching, protracted loss of appetite, even more insomniac nights than usual, and an extended case of writer's block. Not to mention high dudgeon, high anxiety, high horses, too much coffee, and too much smoking.

✍

The day after Christmas I wrote and said, Our festive season here has had its ups and downs so far.

I told you that my friend Michelle's partner, Adam, had to be rushed to the hospital by ambulance on Christmas morning because he'd suffered a stroke at the breakfast table. It turned out to have been a small one and he was back home now, but it was a stroke nonetheless, and we were all very worried about him.

I told you that two days before Christmas, my friend Lorraine's little dog had accidentally eaten ant poison and had to be rushed to the vet to have her stomach pumped out. They kept her over-night for observation but now she's fine.

I told you I'd nearly been rear-ended in a snowstorm on my way to Kate's house for Christmas dinner. I said, It was a close call!

I said, I do hope the rest of the season will pass without any more unforeseen calamities.

I didn't mention the Christmas present from you, which I hadn't yet received. I assumed it would come in a day or two, if not before New Year's, then shortly after.

You said, Thank you so much for your letter! It was so great to receive!

You made no mention of Michelle or Adam or Lorraine's little dog, no mention of strokes or poison or close calls.

You made no mention of the present either.

Every day I waited for the mailman. Every day he did not bring me a present.

A month later I said, You told me you were going to send me a Christmas present, but it still hasn't arrived. I wonder if it's been lost in the mail?

You did not reply.

✑

It occurs to me now that, while trying to make sense of what I took to be signs engendered in teeny-tiny black-and-white plastic cows, recalcitrant crossword puzzle clues, mislaid playing cards, newspaper horoscopes, fortune cookie sayings, a fox crossing the road, pigeons cooing thirty years ago, I missed all the real signs that were there all along.

What was I thinking?

Stupid stupid stupid.

What is wrong with me that I could so consistently take every little crumb you tossed my way and turn it into a full-fledged cake (a three-tiered wedding cake no less, with butter-cream icing sculpted into curlicues and rosebuds, and a pair of kissing porcelain figurines on the top that looked just like you and me)?

What is wrong with me that every time you gave me an inch, I would take a mile?

What is wrong with me that I could keep believing we would end up together someday despite all mounting evidence to the contrary?

What is wrong with me that the harder you tried to get away from me, the harder I tried to hang on to you?

What is wrong with me that I could allow myself to be so pathetically blinded by love . . . not by your obviously dwindling love for me, but by my increasingly desperate love for you?

What is wrong with me that I could mistake any of this for love in the first place?

Kate and Michelle are always telling me not to beat myself up over this whole fiasco. They remind me that every single person in the world has been stupid in the name of love at one time or another.

I say, Some of us more than others.

They hug me.

I cry.

They say, Let she who is without stupidity cast the first stone!

They remind me that if love is not exactly blind, then certainly it is a master of magical thinking, a wizard at seeing only what it wants to see, a virtuoso at hearing only what it wants to hear, and an unrivaled genius at revising reality to suit itself.

They hug me again.

I cry some more.

☞

I said, I want and need to know exactly what is going on with you. True to form, I will now ask you some questions and then you, also true to form, probably will not answer them.

True to form, you did not.

✍

I said, I am so tired of being ignored.
You did not reply.

✍

I said, I am so tired of being stonewalled.
You did not reply.

✍

I said, I am so tired of trying to make myself heard and under-stood in these long anguished letters to which you so seldom reply. What was once a meaningful dialogue has now become a tortured monologue.
You did not reply.

✍

I said, I am so tired of being humiliated by your silence.
You did not reply.

✍

I said, Do you want me to love you or not?
You did not reply.

✍

I am thinking about how here I was in my city, always explain-ing myself, always examining myself and my feelings and you and your feelings in such excruciating and extended (or should I say "distended"?) detail that Kate and Michelle referred to this as me "getting out my dental tools."

I am thinking about how here I was in my city, always seeking answers, clarity, certainty, truth. And there you were in your city, always being vague and evasive, slippery and ambiguous, always dodging, deflecting, and dissembling, always equivocating, hedging, and beating around the bush.

In retrospect, I see now that, while here I was in my city being true to my nature, there you were in your city being true to yours.

✍

Long after my patience had rather obviously run out, still you were always thanking me for it.

You said, I thank you so much for your patience, which you have always been so gracious in giving.

(It occurs to me now that perhaps you were being sarcastic. But at the time, I didn't read it that way, sarcasm being so much more my bailiwick than yours.)

At the time, I said, Thank you. I may not be as patient as you think I am. I've never thought of myself as a patient person . . . but thank you anyway. Now I say: I am not patient. I am not gracious. I have nothing more to give.

✍

I didn't send you any of the newspaper horoscopes that were the most helpful to me. Instead, I cut them out, taped them into my Day-Timer, and kept them to myself.

MINE: Some people seem to be under the impression that you are easily manipulated, and you must go out of your way to prove them wrong. Don't worry if you go a bit over the top today—better that than not doing anything at all. Yours is a cardinal sign, which means you should be the one giving the orders.

MINE: Don't be surprised if someone whose support you thought you could count on disappoints you today. You may be shocked, but the signs have been there for quite some time—you missed them because your relationship blinded you to reality. At least now you know their true colors.

MINE: Fate has a way of bringing the right experience at the right time. If you bear this thought in mind, you are more likely to make recent events work in your favor. While others are wailing that life is unfair, you will be quietly going about your business in a state of calm, even joyful, acceptance.

MINE: Things are looking up for you. You just need to hang in there a little while longer to ride out the storm that has been brewing. Friends are a continued source of support. Soon you will make the breakthrough in understanding that will transform your life and help you make the most of your potential.

I am thinking about how when someone treats you badly, it makes you feel badly about yourself. Especially if that someone happens to be someone you love, someone who professes to love you too. It makes you doubt yourself. It makes you wonder if maybe somehow you deserve it, or maybe it's all your fault that things have gone wrong. It makes you obsess about all your own failings and inadequacies, and how you can change yourself to make things right again. It makes you think that if only you could turn yourself into a better person, then he would have to love you the way you love him, and then . . . eventually . . . then . . . finally . . . then . . . in the end . . . you would both be happy.

✍

I am thinking about how often I hated myself for loving you.

I am thinking about how it proved to be a very short leap from thinking, I am crazy about you, to thinking, I am just plain crazy.

✍

Write about something that was stolen.
Write about something that has yet to happen.
Write about something you would do differently.
Write about something you want but cannot have.
Write about something that belongs to someone else.
Write about something you have never done and never will now.
Write about something you have done and are ashamed of.

✍

Every time I ranted and raved at you by e-mail, I'd end up writing back again before you had a chance to reply, writing back again in half an hour, an hour, two, or three, apologizing for my previous e-mail, which, I said, I knew had been overwrought and overly emotional and over the top. Every time, I ended up apologizing for whining, for complaining, for being so cranky, so demanding, so damned *difficult*.

Then I'd have to write back again a third time to apologize for apologizing.

I said, I wish there was a Take Back button on my computer that was as easy to click on as the Send button. But . . . alas . . . there is not.

I said, Perhaps I should have written a light and breezy note instead of admitting that I'm feeling so upset and hurt.

I said, I'm so sorry. My brain is addled . . . by love, lack of sleep, blocked sinuses, a difficult weekend here, by feeling that you are a million miles away. Plus, when I'm not writing, I do get more than a little squirrelly!

I said, I'm so sorry. Please forgive me for adding to the pressures you are under.

I said, I'm so sorry. I know I was being more than a little self-absorbed.

I said, I'm so sorry. I hope you weren't offended by what I said.

I said, I'm so sorry. I'm trying so hard, but I'm frustrated.

You said, I could never be offended by anything you say . . . and I can certainly understand your frustration. Please do not hold back from saying anything to me or communicating as often as you wish. I always welcome your thoughts and your insights. I miss them so much . . . when there are these reoccurring gaps.

You said, Our story has multiple layers and the chapters are still unfolding. You said it was okay for me to be angry. You said I could say anything . . . absolutely anything . . . to you, and it would be all right.

You said, In our situation, there is no guidebook to follow, no instruction manual to study.

You said, It is a work-in-progress.

I did not say, Too much work, too little progress.

✍

I said, I am sorry. About everything.

I said, I am so emotional, also obsessive, neurotic, anxious, overly sensitive, easily hurt, easily upset, sometimes nasty and bitchy, and, at the moment, very depressed. I am now trying another kind of medication which I hope will work better than the last one.

I said, We are so different. How can we possibly be soul mates?

Two weeks went by. Two long, sad, infuriating weeks in which you did not reply.

Finally, you did.

Finally, you said, I was just now able to open your last letter.

Finally, you said, Please don't be so hard on yourself.

✍

You said, We will be okay if we keep our expectations in perspective.

I said, Then tell me exactly what you expect from me.

You did not reply.

I said, What do you want from me now?

165

You did not reply.

I said, I think in many ways we have both been indulging in an excess of self-delusion.

You said, Work here has been interesting and intense . . .

☛

I said, Over the past year and a half, there have been so many things I've had to accept about this situation, whether I liked it or not. But the one thing I *cannot* accept is feeling that you aren't being straight with me, that you're withholding your feelings, your honest emotions, your own true self.

I said, I can only know what you tell me.

You said I should not expect you to be forthcoming about anything that was going on there.

☛

Once you said you didn't like the idea of me talking about you to my friends. All men say this. All women do it.

As time went on, some of my friends got tired of this topic. They stopped asking about you, and they implied that I was wallowing in my own misery. They were understandably impatient with me. They suggested a new man, a new project, a new hobby, a new haircut. They suggested therapy.

But, wallowing or not, Kate and Michelle stuck with me no matter how long or how often I went on and on about you. They were always supportive and they never seemed to grow tired of my interminable obsession with dissecting the disintegration of our relationship. I apologized to both of them for my single-minded preoccupation.

I said I knew I was a one-trick pony these days. They laughed and agreed, and then we talked about you some more.

The more questions you did not answer, the more hours I logged on the phone with them, the three of us trying to answer the questions ourselves. It was relationship by committee. It was all speculation, and we could do it for hours and hours.

This took so much longer than it would have if only you had just answered the questions yourself.

We are all three of us big phone talkers. We are all three of us writers and very fond of words. We were all three of us frustrated and fit to be tied. We could not for the life of us follow this approach/avoidance dance you were performing. We took to punctuating our lengthy discussions about you with the words "dot dot dot," invariably followed by outraged uproarious laughter.

We called you "The Artful Dodger" and we were collectively mad at you most of the time.

In the early days, Kate often said, Keep steadily on.

I thought this was a wise and lyrical piece of advice, so I took it as my new mantra. Each night when I went to bed alone, I chanted this phrase to myself in a concerted effort to erase and replace those other phrases that usually circled through my head in an endless loop: "I love you . . . I miss you . . . I am so afraid . . ."

I liked Kate's phrase so much that I shared it with you.

You said, Yes, that is a perfect phrase! Beautiful . . . brilliant!

But then you never could get it straight. Every time you tried to say it to me, it came out wrong.

You said, Remember, we must keep moving steadily forward . . .

You said, Yes, we must keep going onward . . .

167

You said, No matter what happens, we must push on.

For a while, Kate was more patient with you than I was. She advised me to bide my time. She said, It will all come clear in the end. It will all work out sooner or later. Just remember: you're a "sooner" kind of girl and he's a "later" kind of guy.

Frequently, Michelle said, For FUCK'S sake!!!!!!!!

Her profane vigor was contagious. Soon enough we were all swearing at you.

Later: Michelle said, I think he's a fucking psychopath!

By this time, not only was I talking to Michelle and Kate about you for hours on the phone, but I'd also started reading your e-mails aloud to both of them. Sometimes I just forwarded your messages to them directly, and then, in true writerly fashion, we would deconstruct them word by word later on.

If it bothered you to think I was talking to them about you, I could just imagine how upset you'd be if you knew I was sending them your e-mails too. It gave me great pleasure to contemplate your distress.

Equally, if not more, pleasurable was our three-way elaboration of my revenge fantasy of traveling to your city and appearing unannounced in your office. I would wear my tightest skirt and a skimpy top and my fancy-dancy high-heeled boots.

Michelle suggested this would be better executed while naked.

Kate said, Naked, yes, but keep the boots.

I would tiptoe through the maze of gray cubicles until I found you.

I imagined that you would be sitting at your computer with your back to me and I would stand there silently until you felt my eyes boring into the back of your head and then you would turn around and there I'd be in all my splendor with a grin on my face, one hand on my hip, and the other brandishing a sheaf of unanswered e-mails.

Kate said, A fistful of condoms.

Michelle said, A hand grenade.

Kate suggested it might be more fun to stage my arrival when you were in yet another important meeting surrounded by your colleagues, your clients, and your boss.

Michelle said, Yes, and then you could leap up on the conference table in those gorgeous boots and stomp on his fingers while strangling him with a telephone cord.

Perfect! I said, laughing so hard I was nearly in tears.

Kate and Michelle together said, Can we come too?

I said, Of course! It wouldn't be the same without you! We'll bring along a video camera and record the whole thing for posterity!

Invigorating and satisfying though this fantasy might be, in reality the closest I ever came to doing anything of the sort was sending a text message from my cellphone to your computer. One of the preset messages, it said simply, On my way.

You did not reply.

An hour later I sent another of the canned messages. This one said, Will arrive in 15 minutes.

Another hour passed with no reply from you. By this time, your silence had sucked all the fun out of my little game. I sent you a regular e-mail from my computer. I said, Just fooling around with my phone. Don't worry . . . I'm right here at home as usual.

You wrote right back. You said, Oh, I wondered who those messages were from.

✍🏼

In our collaborative efforts to understand you, we three women bandied about the term *passive-aggressive* more and more frequently. I realized that, much as I'd used this term often enough to categorize and condemn various people I'd encountered over the years, I didn't know precisely what it meant. So I looked it up. Lo and behold . . . there you were!

As I began to read through the list of passive-aggressive traits, what you once referred to as my "alarm bells" began to tinkle with recognition. Soon they were pealing loudly enough to be heard all the way from my city to yours.

- The passive-aggressive man is afraid of intimacy. Mistrustful and guarded, he is out of touch with his own feelings and reluctant to reveal his emotional fragility. He fights his own dependency by trying to control you. He finds a safe haven in denial, avoidance, and studied indifference.
- The passive-aggressive man is an obstructionist. He always makes promises, but he seldom delivers. He will promise to do whatever you ask, but he won't say when, and he'll do it deliberately slowly just to frustrate you. Or maybe he won't do it at all.
- The passive-aggressive man lies and makes excuses for not fulfilling his promises. As a way of wielding power over you, he will withhold information and/or love, choosing to make up a story rather than give you a

straight answer. When caught out in this ruse, he will say that he was only trying to protect you from the truth.

- The passive-aggressive man complains frequently about his misfortunes and blames his problems and failures on conditions beyond his control. To remain above reproach, he will set himself up as a hapless and innocent person who is unable to meet your excessive demands. Feeling put-upon when he has not lived up to his promises or responsibilities, he will then retreat or withdraw completely.

- The passive-aggressive man prides himself on being "a nice guy." He will not confront you directly when there is conflict. Instead, he will try to undermine your confidence through comments and actions that can be explained away if he is challenged. Nothing is ever his fault. He sees himself as a very complicated person whom nobody else can possibly understand.

- The passive-aggressive man is a procrastinator. He has a peculiar sense of time and believes that deadlines don't exist for him. He is selectively forgetful and chronically late. By keeping you waiting, he maintains control and sets the ground rules for the relationship.

- The passive-aggressive man is a master of ambiguity, mixed messages, and sitting on fences. He never says what he means. After he has told you something, you may still walk away wondering what he actually said.

And so it appeared that, contrary to what you'd once said, there really was an instruction manual for our "situation."

Unfortunately for me, I had come upon it lamentably late in the game.

✍

After I jubilantly shared this passive-aggressive information with Michelle and Kate, Michelle said, No matter how you handled things, it would still have ended up exactly the same.

I found this very consoling.

Also liberating.

✍

I am thinking about how, although I had no inhibitions about telling Kate and Michelle all the juicy and damning details of my difficulties with you, I seldom said much to them about my inability to write while all of this was going on. Somehow my struggles with writer's block were just too private to talk about.

The only way I could explain it was to tell them there was only one story in the world for me at the moment, and *this* story, *our* story, was the one story that I could not possibly write.

Being writers themselves, they understood immediately.

Kate said, When real life is so *large*, fiction seems so small and irrelevant.

Michelle said, Someday the words will come back to you, and then you'll know exactly what you have to say.

I said, I realize I've been a very slow learner here as far as coming to understand how much things have changed between us. I think I get the picture now.

You said, You don't understand . . .

I said, Yes, I do. Finally, yes, I do.

I said, Finally I understand that the relationship I've been having with you is entirely different from the relationship you've been having with me.

Grow up, I tell myself.

Get over it, I tell myself.

Get on with your life, I tell myself.

What goes around comes around, I tell myself.

People get what they deserve, I tell myself a thousand times a day.

But I've never been entirely convinced of this, and am not now.

When I say this, I don't know if I'm talking about myself or you.

Write about a time when you pretended to be someone you are not.

I pretended to be patient. I pretended to be calm, wise, serene, understanding, mature, and angelic. I pretended (sometimes) not to be obsessed, desperate, needy, neurotic, pathetic, furious.

I pretended that I love horses even though the only time I've ever been on one was when I was a little girl and I sat on a Shetland pony as big around as he was tall. I was so afraid of him that I cried until my father lifted me down. I have never ridden a horse in my life and do not intend to.

I pretended that I do not have a relative (if only by marriage) who owned a PMU farm and then raised buffalo for burgers, and who made a small fortune from both endeavors.

I pretended that I don't swear much because you often said you found bad language offensive and never used it yourself. (I pretended not to notice that, much as you didn't say those nasty words, you couldn't ever seem to bring yourself to say the word *sex* either.)

I pretended not to notice your grammatical mistakes and awkward writing style.

I pretended to believe that you kept my books on your bedside table.

I pretended that I dreamed about you, night after love-spattered night.

I pretended to love blueberries, thunderstorms, traveling, the great outdoors, and medieval music. I pretended to know what a hurdy-gurdy was.

I pretended to be serious about quitting smoking.

I pretended (for a few days anyway) to be a practitioner of physical fitness.

I pretended not to care whether you sent me a Christmas present or not.

I pretended to be striving for emotional stability in all aspects of my life.

In retrospect, I can only conclude that you pretended to love me.

✍

I said, I am so tired of being let down and disappointed. I want to be able to count on you, but I've learned over time that this is not a good idea. I am tired, so damn tired, of being treated as if I were the least important thing in your life. Everybody has their limits and I have reached mine. Clearly, there is no room for me in your life and you're not willing to make room.

You said, I am resigned to the fact that I have failed to meet your expectations . . .

I said, Stop talking to me about my expectations. You have expectations too. You've just never bothered to tell me what they are.

✍

You said, The scenario we set each other up for was so far beyond anything we could of envisioned.

I did not say, The scenario *you* set *me* up for was so far beyond anything I could have envisioned.

✍

You said, We will have to help each other through this.

I said, I do not want your help. I just want peace. I'm too old to be carrying on like this, too old to be thrashing around like a big fish in so much pain and turmoil all the time. Normal life seems long ago and far away. I just want to have my old simple solitary life back.

I said, I feel like I've been under a spell, and now I want to wake up and turn back into myself.

✍

The next day was Valentine's Day.

You said, Greetings to you on this day. With best wishes . . . take care there.

I did not reply.

✍

I said, I've laid it all on the line as clearly as I can. Now I will stop. If you want to continue with this, you will have to tell me why . . . openly, honestly, and truthfully. So . . . whatever happens next is up to you.

Half an hour later, I wrote again and said, And if you don't want to continue with this, please have the courage to say so. As I've said so many times before, I do not want or need to be protected. Please do me the honor of telling me the truth for a change.

An hour later, I wrote once more and said, I shouldn't have said that what happens next is up to you. It's not. It's up to me.

Two weeks went by. You did not reply.

To Kate and Michelle, I fumed, Good God! I can't even break up with him properly!

Finally, you wrote back.

Finally, you said, I have been out of the office, working in various locations around the city . . . and so just saw your notes today. Summer staff and projects are now underway here . . . exciting times!

✍

I said, It has been my experience in life that if you push a person away long enough and often enough, eventually they will go. You have been pushing me away for months, and I have been steadfastly refusing to go. But now I think it's time I did.

I said, For my own self-preservation, I have to find a way to become as distant from you as you have become from me.

I said, Maybe this will be better for you, too, as you will no longer feel obligated to be in touch with me when you have so many other more important things to do.

You said, I feel so genuinely awful right now . . . .

You said you felt sick, ashamed, disgusted with yourself for the harm you had caused me due to your inward-looking stupidity.

You said you were devastated to hear what you had put me through. (As if this were the first you had heard of my pain.)

You did not say, Please don't leave me.

You did not say, Please don't give up on this.

You did not say, I couldn't bear to lose you again.

You did not say, I cannot live without you.

I did not say, Don't talk to me about devastation. I've cornered the market on devastation. As well as on many other conditions that also begin with the letter *d*.

Desolation.

Desperation.

Depression.

Despond.

Despair.

I said, It didn't have to be this hard.
You said, I know I continue to disappoint you.
I said, Yes. You do.

You said, I feel like a loser in many ways.
I did not say, You feel like a loser because you are.

I said, When you walked back into my life after thirty years,
I thought I was older and wiser. Apparently I am only older.
Everybody knows there's no fool like an old fool.
I said I felt that you had played me for a fool in many ways.
You did not deny this.

You said, My feelings of love, admiration, respect, fondness,
affection, and genuine caring for you have always been and
always will be within me . . . . . for all time. I believe that, despite
all this recent upset, our lifelong friendship will always endure,
transcending time and all the twists and turns that life may bring.

I said, I do not want to be your friend.

✍

I said, I hope you've thrown away everything I ever sent you, everything you have that has anything to do with me. I want to wipe this whole thing from living memory forever.

You said, I would never throw away anything you gave me. I will always treasure and cherish the best of what we shared.

Clearly you are not afflicted, as I am (as most people are), by that retroactive phenomenon that causes the eventual end of the story to change the beginning and everything that has happened in between. Clearly you are immune to the infectious contamination of the happy past by the unhappy present.

Clearly you are not aware of the fact that, when all is said and done, I will have to say I never loved you at all, not even the first time thirty years ago.

✍

You said, You have been through so much with me and I will always deeply regret this.

I did not reply.

I did not say, Don't talk to me about regret. I've cornered the market on that too.

✍

You said, Somehow I will make this up to you.

I said, I don't want to have anything more to do with you ever again.

This may not have been entirely true before I said it. But once I did . . . it was.

I

You said, I am pretty much devastated for good now . . .

You said, I hate myself . . .

I decided to get on my high horse and ride.

I said, I suppose there are many good reasons why you might hate yourself, but I would not presume to know what they are. I would just say that self-hatred accomplishes nothing. What is required is action and accountability. There are also probably many good reasons why you might feel "pretty much devastated for good now" . . . but again, I do not presume to know what they are. I do not presume to know anything about you really. I do know that, as time passes, you will recover. That's what people do. That's what human nature is all about. Rescue and recovery. After all, what is the alternative?

You did not reply.

For once, I did not expect you to.

Much as you love horses, I knew you would not love *this* horse: my high horse prancing with nostrils flared, mane flying, tail twitching, whites of the eyes showing, also possibly the teeth.

✍

Last week it was my birthday. I had a wonderful time here with my friends. We laughed a lot and ate too much of an elegant chicken salad with raisins, pine nuts, and grapes, followed by strawberry shortcake for dessert. They gave me books and bubble bath and funny cards. I bought myself a card too, one selected especially in your honor (in honor of your silence, in honor of your absence).

On the front, superimposed on a grainy photograph of a man's muscular, but headless, torso, it said: *He ate right, exercised regularly, and he still died.*

Inside it said: *What's up with that? Eat cake.*

We did.

✍

The day after my birthday I went through my whole house and rounded up every single thing that had anything to do with you.

First I dismantled the little shrine-like shelf I'd made in my bedroom bookcase. There was that fortune cookie saying from my fridge calendar, *Your first love has never forgotten you,* that I'd placed in a small brushed silver frame. There were three photographs of you: one taken here in my backyard, you sitting at the picnic table squinting into the sun after cold chicken and Greek barley salad for lunch; two shots of you standing in front of the luxury hotel, one in which you look very sad and the other in which, after my encouragement and insistence, you are sporting a big dopey smile. These two were taken in the winter. There are dirty snowbanks all around and the sky is such a pale blue it looks white. I kept these two photos together in a hinged leather frame that opened like a book. At the bottom of the sad picture I'd taped a quote from the American writer Anne Lamott: *When God is going to do something wonderful, He or She always starts with a hardship; when God is going to do something amazing, He or She starts with an impossibility.*

Next, me being me, I filed our entire e-mail correspondence chronologically in accordion folders. (Of course, I'd printed them all as we went along and, yes, I am a genius at organization!) Stacked in a pile, they were eight inches high. Out of curiosity, I put them on the bathroom scale. They weighed fourteen pounds. I suspect that seven of those inches and thirteen of those pounds are my e-mails to you, with the remaining inch and pound being your e-mails to me.

I gathered up a few books:

Zen and the Art of Falling in Love that I'd bought remaindered at a bookstore in your city the last time we saw each other. And from which I'd sent you several quotes by Zen masters including:

We never ask the meaning of life when we are in love.

Do you have the patience to wait until the mud settles?

We cannot know if it is gold until we see it through the fire.

When you really look for me, you will see me instantly.

A book called *My Boyfriend's Back: True Stories of Rediscovering Love with a Long-Lost Sweetheart* that I never got around to reading and never will now. It is torture enough to look at the section of "Then and Now" pictures in the middle: high school class photos of each couple at the top of each page with the thirty- or forty-years-later wedding pictures below. I should have bought another book instead, one that was a bestseller right then: *He's Just Not That into You.*

And there was also the book Lorraine had recommended: *Reinventing Your Life.* Tried . . . failed.

There were a handful of cards, both funny and sappy, that I'd been collecting and intending to send you:

A photograph of a lavish bed of red and yellow tulips. *Thoughts of you brighten my day . . . So glad you're part of my life.*

A drawing of a dolly, the kind used to move heavy furniture. *You move me . . . in unusual ways.*

A silhouette of a telephone against a dark pink background completely covered with the words *You have no new messages,* repeated in small black print hundreds of times. Inside: *That about sums up my life. How are things with you?*

There was also the only card you ever sent me. Last year for my birthday. A cartoon of a cake on the front, with the words: *Did you make a wish? I did.* Inside it said, *My wish for you is that you always have reasons to smile, favorite memories to look back on, and the very best of times ahead of you.* Even at the time, this struck me as something you could just as well have sent to your sister or your mother or one of your old aunts. But I pushed this thought away and thanked you as profusely as if you'd sent me a diamond ring. I said, You are so thoughtful and kind, you are so good to me, you are the most wonderful man in the world! I can only conclude that you are . . . a doll!

I piled all these things on the kitchen table and sat there staring at the heap for an hour. Trying to decide what to do with them: these once-treasured mementos now become nothing more than detritus, these scraps and fragments of yet another misbegotten romance, the flotsam and jetsam of yet another broken heart. Trying to decide how to dispose of all that was left of my dream of me and you.

I considered hauling everything out to the backyard and setting it on fire. Symbolic and satisfying though this might be, it still seemed a bit melodramatic even for me. Besides, there's a burning ban in effect in the city just now and, with my luck, one of my neighbors would call the police or the fire department or both.

I considered tossing the lot into a big green garbage bag and putting it out with the trash, but that didn't seem ceremonial enough, and besides, most of it was recyclable.

Neither of these options, the fire or the trash, satisfied the pack-rat side of my nature anyway.

Although I'd said I hoped you would throw away everything I'd ever given you, everything you had that had anything to do with me, I had no serious intention of doing the same myself.

So I went downstairs and rummaged around in the basement until I found a big blue plastic storage tub that could be easily divested of its current contents (a macramé plant hanger, a set of kitchen canisters with ducks on them, three old sweaters, an inflatable bath pillow, and a see-through shower curtain) and used as a repository for all this junk.

I packed the items into it, one by one.

The photographs.

The e-mails, all fourteen pounds of them.

The four letters from thirty years ago and the cigar box in which I'd kept them.

The *Dancing in the Moonlight* CD.

The books.

The cards.

The Tuscany calendar.

The train schedule between my city and yours.

The three stalks of purple freesia that I'd taken from the luxury hotel the first time we slept together. I had tried to dry them properly, but now they were all just crumpled and rotten.

The ticket stub for an art exhibit we were supposed to attend together but at the last minute you couldn't make it and I went alone and cried in front of Tom Thomson's famous painting of a northern forest with black pine trees in the foreground and a still river shimmering in the background. A security guard watched me impassively the whole time, with his arms folded across his chest.

A brochure from the hotel. Also monogrammed writing paper and notepads, four empty matchbooks, three blank postcards, and half a dozen monogrammed envelopes, into one of which I'd slipped the ace of hearts playing card I'd found in the corner store parking lot.

A bar of fragrant wild honey soap you gave me that I never used because I wanted to keep it forever, and an empty bag that had contained a pound of expensive gourmet free-trade coffee on which you'd written, Hope this tastes good! These, the soap and the coffee, were the birthday gifts you'd given me with that card last year.

An empty box from a dozen handmade chocolate truffles that we had shared mouth to mouth.

The bottle of Obsession perfume, almost empty now, used as a pillow spray at first, and then as a bathroom deodorizing spray.

The special notepaper I used whenever I sent you something by regular mail. Prettily patterned in four different styles, each bearing an inspirational message:

Believe in the wisdom of your heart.

Sweet Destiny: There is significance in every moment.

Life Is a Journey: Dream, explore, and find peace in life's adventure.

Time brings a kind of wisdom only the heart can understand.

I also put in two shirts you'd admired: the turquoise silk one I'd bought especially to please you and had worn the last time I saw you, and the beige one with the rhinestones and the French phrase that I'd bought because our song came on the store Muzak. And then I put in a third, because one day on the phone you said you'd had a dream about me wearing a blue shirt and sure enough, there I was in a blue shirt. At the time, I took this as yet another sign of how psychically connected we were.

Now I think: Everybody owns at least one blue shirt.

At the last minute, I took all three shirts out of the box and hung them back in my closet. I like them too.

I briefly considered putting in the bottle of Fever nail polish, but then I remembered that you had never actually seen it on my toes anyway. And besides, I've become quite fond of it and seldom go now with naked toenails.

I also thought of putting in my fancy-dancy high-heeled black leather boots that you liked so much, but they cost three hundred dollars and so they remain in my front hall closet.

I put the lid on the box and lugged it back down to the basement. I stashed it in the back room with a dozen other identical plastic tubs containing Christmas decorations, old curtains, jigsaw puzzles, board games, two dozen first-edition Nancy Drew books, twenty years' worth of old calendars, the guest books from both my parents' funerals, and my extensive collection of Barbie dolls.

I turned off the light and closed the door. I reflected on how much larger the box I kept you in now was compared to how small it used to be.

I went back upstairs and had a nap. I turned on the fan, stretched out on the couch, and fell instantly asleep.

I did not awaken until almost four hours later, during which time I did not move, I did not dream, and I did not cry.

✍

Of course, I no longer send you the newspaper horoscopes. In fact, I don't even read yours anymore. Now I only read my own, and I still save the best ones in my Day-Timer for future reference.

MINE: Always look forward. Never look back. Tomorrow's new moon in your sign is a wonderful omen of success, but the level of success that you enjoy will be in proportion to your willingness to move on. The limitations and restrictions that have been such a predominant feature of your life recently will slowly begin to fade. No matter how many times you have deceived yourself in the past, you can see with utmost clarity now.

MINE: What's done is done and cannot be undone. If you accept that today, you will feel a great sense of peace and an even greater sense of freedom. Recent events have opened up a world of possibilities and if you can't see them yet, it is only because you are still thinking of the past instead of the future. Remember that it is the future that matters, and the future begins here and now.

MINE: It's a good job you are not the sort to give up easily, because something you have struggled with in the past will start to come easily to you today. By the end of the week you will be flying. A project you lost enthusiasm for a while back will start to interest you again and this time, it seems, you will make a huge success of it.

✍

I am thinking about how in one of your last letters, you said, I am beside myself if I have had an impact on your writing too . . . . I, please, urge you to write . . . If what we have gone through can be some of what gives you subject matter to write about . . . perhaps that would be one path out of this . . .

At the time, I did not reply.

At the time, I was at a loss for words, struck dumb by an acute case of aphasia, a condition that my dictionary defines as: *the loss of the ability to express or understand language, owing to brain damage.*

But now I say: You are arrogant and patronizing.

Now I say: Your grammar is bad.

Now I say: Hell hath no fury.
Now I say: Be careful what you wish for.

✍

I am thinking about your wife.

I am thinking about the one and only time I met her, and you were so uxorious, so solicitous, so obsequious. You were like a gymnast, turning yourself inside out and upside down to please her.

This was long before things got complicated.

But even then, we were none of us meeting each other's eyes.

Maybe even then, she knew what was coming.

Maybe she knew before we did.

Maybe she knew you better than you thought she did, better than I did, better than you knew yourself.

✍

Now I say: It would appear that I am no longer at a loss for words.

✍ ✍ ✍

Acknowledgments

The particulars of crossword puzzles, horoscopes, cartoons, and newspaper articles were drawn from my daily reading of the Ontario edition of *The Globe and Mail*.

The writer's block books listed on page 8 are all actual books and, although I make some fun of them here, they are interesting and useful, each in its own way. The various instructions and exercises that appear here in italics have been culled from these books.

The addresses of the websites mentioned on pages 65 to 66 are as follows:

The Sound Archive of the British Library: http://www.bl.uk/collections/sound-archive/nsa.html

Save the Mustangs Foundation: http://www.savethemustangfoundation.com

The Archive of Misheard Lyrics: http://www.kissthisguy.com

The information about the passive-aggressive man was originally found on the Passive Aggressive Helping Hand website at http://www.passiveaggressive.homestead.com. For further reading, see Dr. Scott Wetzler's book, *Living with the Passive Aggressive Man: Coping with Hidden Aggression — From the Bedroom to the Boardroom*, published by Simon & Schuster, 1992.

About the author

2 Author Biography
5 A Conversation with Diane
   Schoemperlen

Ideas,
interviews
& features

About the book

11 "On Writing *At A Loss For Words*," by
    Diane Schoemperlen

Read on

14 "Are You Obsessed? Eight Telltale Signs
    of Romantic Obsession," by Diane
    Schoemperlen
17 Further Reading
19 Web Detective

Diane Schoemperlen

Author Biography

DIANE SCHOEMPERLEN was born and raised in Thunder Bay, Ontario. She was the only child of older parents, neither of whom had finished high school. Her father was a weighman in a grain elevator and her mother ran a post-office outlet in a small drugstore. Diane always loved books, and from an early age, she dreamed of becoming a writer. As a child, she penned stories inspired by the Trixie Belden and Nancy Drew mystery series she collected. Because no one else in her family shared her interest in books and writing, she used to wonder if she was adopted. . . . She wasn't!

Diane's interest in creative writing continued throughout her school and university years. After graduating from Lakehead University in 1976, she spent the summer at the Banff Centre studying with such well-known literary figures as W. O. Mitchell and Alice Munro. For the first time in her life, Diane was surrounded by people who shared her interest in things literary and who encouraged her writing efforts. Shortly after, she pulled up stakes and moved first to Banff, and then, a few months later, to Canmore, Alberta. There, she continued writing while supporting herself with a variety of jobs—including bank teller, newspaper reporter, typesetter, and even avalanche researcher. One of her little-known early publications was an article titled "Avalanche Fatalities in North American Mountaineering," published in the *Canadian Alpine Journal*.

Diane soon began publishing short fiction in such literary journals as *Descant, The Malahat Review, Event, Quarry,* and *Canadian Fiction Magazine,* and by 1983 she was featured in *Coming Attractions* as a notable new writing talent. Her first book, *Double Exposures* (1984), established her trademark wit and ironic style, and her second book, *Frogs and Other Stories* (1986), won the Writers Guild of Alberta Award for Excellence.

In the summer of 1986, Diane traveled east to teach a one-week course at Queen's University in Kingston. Again she found herself surrounded by people who shared her literary interests. At the time, Kingston was home to such writers as Bronwen Wallace, Tom Marshall, and David Helwig. She liked the city so much that she decided to move there with her one-year-old son and ten-year-old cat. In the years that followed, she taught creative writing at St. Lawrence College and the Kingston School of Writing, and led many workshops throughout Ontario.

Hockey Night in Canada, published in 1987, propelled Diane into the ranks of the country's most talented short story writers. "Red Plaid Shirt," which appeared in *Saturday Night*, received the 1989 silver National Magazine Award for Fiction. An adaptation of that short story has since been performed as a one-woman play across Western Canada. *The Man of My Dreams*, her 1990 short fiction collection, was shortlisted for both the Governor General's Award and the Trillium Award.

Diane's first novel, *In the Language of Love* (1994), received critical acclaim. Shortlisted for the *Books in Canada*/W. H. Smith First Novel Award and chosen by the *Toronto Star* as one of the year's ten best novels, it has since been published internationally. Schoemperlen's *Forms of Devotion* (1998), a unique collection of illustrated stories featuring an interplay ▶

Author Biography *(continued)*

of language and images, won her the Governor General's Award for Fiction. This book, along with *In the Language of Love*, has been performed on stage by Threshold Theatre.

Between 2001 and 2004, Diane published her second novel, *Our Lady of the Lost and Found*, the short story collection *Red Plaid Shirt: Stories New and Collected*, and her first book of non-fiction, *Names of the Dead: An Elegy for the Victims of September 11*. *At A Loss For Words*, her third novel, was published in 2008.

In 2007, Diane was honored with the prestigious Marian Engel Award, presented annually to a female Canadian writer for a body of work. She has been described variously as "one of the most vibrant and original voices in our literature," "incredibly intelligent and observant" and "innovative." Her work has been published in the United States, the United Kingdom, Germany, Sweden, France, Spain, China, and Korea.

Diane Schoemperlen lives in Kingston with her son, Alexander, her partner, Dale Thompson, their little dogs, Nelly and Maggie, and their three cats, Max, Sammy, and Buster.

To listen to a Prosecast interview with the author, visit **www.foursevens.com/prosecast/page/2/**

❧

A Conversation with Diane Schoemperlen

When did you start writing, and how?

I cannot remember a time when I wasn't writing, or wanting to. My mother loved to tell the story of how back before I could read, I used to haul her cookbooks from the box under my bed where she kept them (why there, I don't know) and tell her stories from them, pretending to read. I have always wanted to be a writer. For a long time, I read anything I could get my hands on, Harlequin romances included. As I grew older, obviously my tastes changed! I don't know exactly why I began with short stories—probably because, like many people, I was under the misconception that short stories were easier to tackle because they were short. I wrote stories for a long time, partly because I think I would have considered it presumptuous and preposterous to imagine that I could write a novel.

> " I have always wanted to be a writer. "

How did the publication of your first book, *Double Exposures* (1984), change your life?

At the time, I was living in Canmore, Alberta, and working in a convenience store. The day the first copies of the book arrived, I decided to go out and celebrate. I was supposed to work that evening, so I called in sick and went to a local watering hole with a group of my friends. Later in the evening, after we'd had many pitchers of beer, the husband of the ▶

5

A Conversation with Diane Schoemperlen (*continued*)

manager of the convenience store showed up at the bar. The next day, I was fired.

But apart from losing my job, the publication of my first book made me believe in myself as a real writer. Prior to that, I had published quite a few stories in literary journals, but if someone asked me what I did, I could only say, usually while shuffling my feet and avoiding eye contact, "I write." After the book's publication, I could say, "I'm a writer."

Where does a piece of fiction usually begin for you?

Most often, a piece of fiction begins with an idea about form and structure: for instance, the idea of writing a story with pictures, or a story told in e-mails, or a story alternating between fact and fiction. Sometimes a story begins with a sentence that is stuck in my head. Sometimes this is a sentence of my own. (My story "Forms of Devotion" came from this first sentence: "The faithful are everywhere.") Sometimes the sentence is from something I've read. After reading "The Catechist," by Donald Barthelme, this sentence lodged in my brain: "There is never a day, never a day, on which we do not have this conversation." Do not be surprised if someday I publish a story called "Never a Day"!

My earlier collections of stories were written one story after another until there were enough stories to make a book. I had no overall theme or concept in mind as I wrote.

> **Sometimes a story begins with a sentence that is stuck in my head.**

But *Forms of Devotion* was conceived as a book from the beginning.

Alice Munro, under whom you studied, is one of your favorite writers. What do you most admire about her work? How does your work differ from hers?

I have always admired Alice Munro's ability to turn seemingly ordinary characters and situations into something marvelous and mysterious and meaningful. I also love her attention to detail. I think that she, like me, is a very visual writer, fond of describing things. I also think we share a deep and abiding awareness of the irony in the world. As for how my work is different, I think I use more experimental structures than she does (or than she did in her earlier stories). She is such a master of the short story form that I don't even feel comfortable comparing myself to her! I still have so much to learn from her. Rereading her stories is, for me, always an inspiration.

Your work has been hailed as experimental and unconventional. What do you consider to be the most innovative aspect of your writing?

I suppose it would be my adventures with form and structure. I do like to push the story envelope as far as I can. I find it exciting and challenging and fun to turn some of the conventions of fiction on their heads and see what happens. Again, I am not always conscious of doing that while I'm doing it, ▶

> " I do like to push the story envelope as far as I can. "

A Conversation with Diane Schoemperlen
(*continued*)

but afterwards I can step back and see what I've done. Sometimes the experiment works and sometimes it doesn't.

You have said that you "don't have a real definition of what a story is." Can you explain what you mean by that?

I think of Flannery O'Connor who, when asked to define a short story, said it was a question "inspired by the devil who tempts textbook publishers." Then she went on to say what a story is not: a story is not a joke, an anecdote, a lyric rhapsody in prose, a case history, or a reported incident. I would agree with all of these nots and still be hard-pressed to come up with a definition of what a story is. I use the word *story* in the loosest possible sense. I think of a story as telling somebody about something. I like the way my son, when he was small, used to tell me the stories of his day. He would say, "And then . . . and then . . . and then . . . and then." This is a good way to think of a story: the telling of then and then and then. I don't think about labels, categories, definitions, and so on when I'm writing. I think I would be paralyzed if I did. I still remember, word for word, something that I read almost twenty years ago in an article by a woman named Josephine Jacobsen in *The Writer* magazine: "Like the centipede, which, questioned as to its method of locomotion, never moved again, the writer, considering the how of what he is doing as he does it, is lost."

" This is a good way to think of a story: the telling of then and then and then. "

What is the best piece of advice you ever heard?

The best piece of advice I ever heard was actually the worst piece of advice I ever heard. When I was a student at Lakehead University back in the1970s, my creative writing professor said, "A short story must never be written in the present tense." For many years I believed him. But, eventually, I got over it. This reminds me that there are no hard-and-fast rules in writing fiction.

Can you describe your typical writing routine?

My ideal writing routine is to write from early morning until early afternoon. Then after lunch, I like to have a nap, then do all that other stuff that is always demanding to be done (errands, chores, phone calls, et cetera). I sometimes also like to work in the evening, particularly if I am doing research or copy editing or some such relatively mechanical task.

The beginning of each day is hugely important to me. I begin every day in the same way. I get up early, have coffee and read for an hour or so in my special chair (usually accompanied by my dog and one or two of my three cats). Then I get dressed and get straight to work. If for any reason I cannot have my morning routine, I am grumpy and unproductive for the rest of the day.

What theoretical considerations, if any, underlie your writing? ▶

❝ There are no hard-and-fast rules in writing fiction. ❞

A Conversation with Diane Schoemperlen (*continued*)

Generally speaking, I think the theoretical concerns are best left to the critics. I don't think about theory while I'm writing. It would interfere with the creative process. While actually writing, the only question I am trying to answer is: How can I best tell this story?

I love writing, the physical act of writing. Theories are not so important to me. All I want to do is write. So for me, the current question is always: Why do I have to do all these other things (shopping, cleaning, eating, mowing the lawn, vacuuming, laundry, et cetera) when all I want to do is write?

—*Excerpts reprinted, with permission, from "Eva Tihanyi Speaks with Diane Schoemperlen" (Books in Canada, April 1999) and "12 or 20 Questions with Diane Schoemperlen," by rob mclennan* (http://12or20questions.blogspot.com/2008/05/12-or-20-questions-with-diane.html, May 2008).

❝ I love writing, the physical act of writing. Theories are not so important to me. ❞

On Writing *At A Loss For Words*

by Diane Schoemperlen

One of the questions a writer is asked most frequently is: Where do you get your ideas? For me, ideas come from anywhere and everywhere, most often by chance. For instance, the idea for my first novel, *In the Language of Love*, came from my accidental discovery of a list of the 100 words of the Standard Word Association Test used in diagnostic psychological testing. My short story "How Deep Is the River?" (from *Forms of Devotion*) grew out of a conversation overheard on a train. The idea for my second novel, *Our Lady of the Lost and Found*, came from television, when I watched a documentary about visions of the Virgin Mary and other mysterious religious phenomena.

The idea for *At A Loss For Words* also came from television. One day I saw *Oprah* (yes, I confess that I do occasionally watch *Oprah* and sometimes *Dr. Phil* also). She was interviewing Donna Hanover, former wife of New York City mayor Rudy Giuliani. Hanover had been happily reunited with her high school sweetheart, and she was speaking about *My Boyfriend's Back*, the book she had written about her own and other people's experiences of rekindling a long-lost love. Several other couples who had been reunited after many years and were now living happily ever after were featured on the show. Perhaps I am a cynic, but it occurred to me that not all of these rekindled romance stories could be so perfect and happy. ▶

> " For me, ideas come from anywhere and everywhere, most often by chance. "

On Writing *At A Loss For Words* (*continued*)

At A Loss For Words began as a short story with the subtitle "27 Reasons Why I Cannot Write Today." Anyone who knows my work will know how much I love lists. This story was written in the form of a list, with each short section numbered sequentially. The writing came easily to me, and so the story, once launched, grew quickly. I enjoyed putting in the parts about horoscopes, crossword puzzles, and, of course, writer's block.

One of the most important themes of the story is the nature of communication. The narrator is a writer, a communicator, but after she becomes involved with this man, she is stricken by writer's block. She loses her ability to communicate with anyone but him . . . and he's not talking back! The phenomenon of the e-mail romance is particular to our age. The medium is easy, accessible, and immediate. But it has its limitations, too, as the characters in the story soon discover. And it has its dangers. You can read an e-mail over and over again, interpreting it in as many different ways as you like. You can say all kinds of things in an e-mail that you probably wouldn't say if you were face to face with the recipient. Once an e-mail is sent, you cannot take it back.

Soon, the subtitle of the story became "49 Reasons Why I Cannot Write Today," then 77, 120, 150, 163! By this point, I had to admit that what I was writing was no longer a short story. I am an avid reader of short novels and have always wanted to write one, my two earlier novels being in the 300-plus page range. And so *At A Loss For Words* evolved

> " The phenomenon of the e-mail romance is particular to our age. "

into a short novel. By the time I had completed the first full draft of the manuscript, the number in the subtitle was 203! Following the wise advice of my editor, Phyllis Bruce, I dropped the numbering.

The novel is primarily humorous, although of course there are also sad passages and serious questions of moral ambiguity. I wanted to show that even a strong, intelligent, and accomplished woman can become a fool for love.

Are You Obsessed? Eight Telltale Signs of Romantic Obsession

Is he the man of your dreams or the monster of your nightmares? Is he the object of your affection or the subject of your obsession? Sometimes it's hard to tell the difference. If you recognize yourself in four or more of the following telltale signs, chances are you are obsessed!

1. You find yourself having long and meaningful conversations with him when he is not in the room. When he is not in your house. When he is not even in the same city. When watching TV alone in the evening, you find yourself laughing aloud and glancing frequently at the empty expanse of the couch to your left, just checking to see if he is enjoying the program as much as you are.

2. You develop a sudden and compulsive interest in horses, although horses are something to which you have seldom given a second thought. (You do not ever admit that secretly you are afraid of horses.) He is an avid equestrian. You lose your taste for pepperoni pizza, double cheeseburgers and Tim Hortons Iced Capps. You find yourself eating salad and tofu, drinking soy milk and green tea. (You do not ever admit that tofu makes you gag.) He is a dedicated vegetarian. He swears that he has not eaten a single bite of junk food in the last ten years. You believe him.

3. You find yourself subscribing to five different daily horoscopes on the Internet. Each morning, after reading your horoscope in the newspaper, you run to your computer and check the astrology e-mails. Then you decide which one you like the best. You stick it in your Day-Timer and read it many times during the day. You are convinced that the stars know more about your life than you do.

4. You find yourself buying large plastic tubs of fortune cookies at your local Chinese grocery store. (You are relieved to discover that these cookies contain no trans fats, no cholesterol, and no sodium. You ignore the fact that they also contain no protein, no fiber, no calcium, and no vitamins.) You eat two dozen cookies at a single sitting and save the most promising fortunes in a special compartment in your purse. You reread these frequently, whenever you need a little reassurance: "Your qualities overshadow your weaknesses," "Happiness can be achieved through patience and understanding," "The one you love will never let you down." You are convinced that the Chinese know more about your life than you do.

5. You find yourself watching romantic comedies every weekend when he is not available. (This is more often than not. You believe all his excuses.) You sometimes watch four of these movies in a row and cry with happiness at the end of each one. You want to be like the women in these movies. They are beautiful and funny, and everything works out for them eventually, no matter how complicated the situation. Surely the same can be true for you. Surely you deserve ▶

> ❝ You eat two dozen cookies at a single sitting and save the most promising fortunes in a special compartment in your purse. ❞

Are You Obsessed? (*continued*)

a happy ending too. When not watching romantic comedies, you are reading self-help books.

6. When talking to your female friends, you find that you have only one topic: HIM. You dissect everything he said and how charming and romantic he was the last time you saw him. Your friends nod and smile. You weep and wail repeatedly about everything he didn't say and how he was two hours late for dinner. Your friends hug you and hand you more Kleenex while you cry and your mascara runs all over your red and blotchy face. You realize that you cannot speak a single sentence that does not contain his name. You realize that your friends are sick of you. You realize that they love you anyway.

7. Despite all evidence to the contrary, you believe this man will never hurt you.

8. Despite all evidence to the contrary, you believe this man is perfect.

> **You realize that you cannot speak a single sentence that does not contain his name.**

16

Further Reading

*Living with the Passive Aggressive Man:
Coping with Hidden Aggression—from the
Bedroom to the Boardroom,* by Scott
Wetzler, Ph.D.
If the man in my novel sounds more than
passingly familiar, you must read this book!

Heartburn, by Nora Ephron
Based on the author's own experience with
her husband, Carl Bernstein, of Watergate
fame, this book tells the story of a writer who
is seven months' pregnant when she discovers
her husband is in love with another woman.
Heartburn (as the *Chicago Tribune* declared) is
"proof that writing well is the best revenge."

Liar: A Poem, by Lynn Crosbie
I reread this book several times while writing
my novel, and it never failed to inspire me.
The long narrative poem is a brilliant dissec-
tion of passion and pain in a reinvention of
the "confessional" mode.

*The Midnight Disease: The Drive to Write,
Writer's Block, and the Creative Brain,* by
Alice W. Flaherty
A well-researched examination of the myster-
ies of literary creativity and the brain processes
it involves, this book is one that I recommend
to all my writerly friends, whether they are
blocked or not! ▶

Further Reading (*continued*)

New and Selected Poems: Volume One and
Volume Two, by Mary Oliver
Gentle and sharp at the same time, Mary
Oliver is, in my opinion, one of the greatest
poets of all time. Reading a handful of these
poems every day kept me going during the
writing of my novel.

❦

Web Detective

"Epistolary Romance, Digital Style"
http://archive.salon.com/21st/feature/1998/04/cov_27feature.html
This *Salon* article by Jenn Shreve is a personable and serious look at how e-mail has transformed romance in our technological age. As Shreve writes, "The absence of constant feedback makes it easy to bare one's soul without fear of instantaneous rejection. The result is a strong sense of intimacy created in a vacuum."

"Is Online Romance Just Like the Real Thing?"
www.msnbc.msn.com/id/25607240/
In this Q&A advice article, psychiatrist and regular *Today Show* contributor Dr. Gail Saltz advises a woman enmeshed in an online relationship with a man whose wife is in a coma: "Online relationships are breeding grounds for fantasy. If one party resists moving a relationship into the real world, for whatever reason, it will never progress."

My Boyfriend's Back: 50 True Stories of Rediscovering Love with a Long-Lost Sweetheart, by Donna Hanover
www.myboyfriendsback.com
This website for Donna Hanover's book tracks the phenomenon of long-lost sweethearts reuniting happily twenty, thirty, or even forty years later. This has been described as a twenty-first-century relationship trend. ▶

Web Detective (*continued*)

911 Writer's Block
www.webook.com/911writersblock
What do you do when the words dry up and
the mere sight of your computer makes you feel
sick? 911 Writers Block to the rescue! Organized
as a touch-tone telephone pad, this website
allows you to dial exactly what you need. Dial
number one for settings, two for characters,
three for dramatic entrances, four for dialogue,
five to commiserate, and so on. Clever and creative, this site may not cure your block, but at
least you'll have some fun!

To receive updates on author
events and new books by Diane
Schoemperlen, sign up today at
www.authortracker.ca.